'You didn't tell me you had a daughter.'

'I didn't think you'd be interested.'

'Oh, come on, Liz! You told me about your mother and your sister but...'

'I didn't think you'd be interested because you said you didn't like children.'

Jacques frowned. 'When did I say that?'

'Oh, the first time we went out together. And when we met up again this time you obviously hadn't changed. You said you didn't want a family.'

'Yes, but that's different from not liking children. I like other people's children. It's just that...'

Jacques's bleeper was going. 'I've got to go.'

Liz watched him hurrying away down the ward. The [illegible] the bag now, [illegible] he story.

Margaret Barker has enjoyed a variety of interesting careers. A State Registered Nurse and qualified teacher, she holds a degree in French and Linguistics and is a Licentiate of the Royal Academy of Music. As a full-time writer Margaret says, 'Writing is my most interesting career because it fits perfectly into my happy life as a wife, mother and grandmother. My husband and I live in an idyllic sixteenth-century house near the East Anglian coast. Our grown-up children have flown the nest, but they often fly back again, bringing their own young families with them for wonderful weekend and holiday reunions.'

Recent titles by the same author:

DR SOTIRIS'S WOMAN*
DR DEMETRIUS'S DILEMMA*
DR MICHAELIS'S SECRET*

**Greek Island Hospital trilogy*

THE FRENCH SURGEON'S SECRET CHILD

BY
MARGARET BARKER

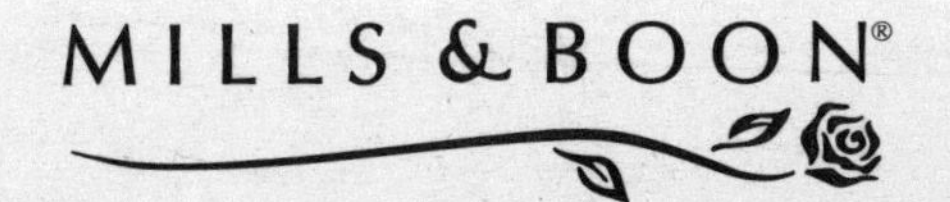

First published in Great Britain 2003
Harlequin Mills & Boon Limited,
Eton House, 18-24 Paradise Road, Richmond, Surrey TW9 1SR

ISBN 0 263 83469 7

Set in Times Roman 10½ on 12 pt.
03-0903-49544

Printed and bound in Spain
by Litografia Rosés, S.A., Barcelona

CHAPTER ONE

THERE was a fisherman sitting in his boat, way out in the middle of the bay. At least, he looked like a fisherman. Liz shielded her eyes from the hot Mediterranean sun so she could get a better look at him. Even wearing her newly purchased designer sunglasses, there was a constant glare that dazzled her.

Better than being back in London, though! Yes, much better. A good decision to apply for this job. Even though she hadn't yet started work at the Clinique de la Côte, Liz was confident she was going to enjoy her work there. From everything that had been said about this brand-new clinic at her interview in London, Liz was certain it was going to be a first-class place for a doctor to work.

She sat down on a warm rock at the edge of the beach, pulling off her sandals and scrunching her toes into the soft sand. Mmm! Happiness was a foot covered in warm sand, the hot sun on your face and that indefinable smell of fresh seaweed tangled in your toes. Seaweed made you so nostalgic, reminding you of childhood holidays out here on the French Mediterranean coast, buckets and spades, sandcastles, Club Mickey…

And she had the whole of the summer to look forward to. It was only July. Loads of time while off duty to wander on the beach each day. This beach…this very special beach. She felt a pang of a very different kind of nostalgia sweeping over her. A definitely adult nostalgia this time, but she tried to banish the poignant memory as quickly as it attempted to claim her thoughts.

The man in the boat was restarting the engine. It spluttered into life and propelled the boat towards the shore. She could see the man was alone. Why was she so interested in him? Was it because he brought back memories of that other man? That man who'd stolen her heart on this very beach and never returned it? Had turned her life around, made her take sweeping decisions about where she'd been going and—?

Hang on a minute! The outline of the man at the helm of the boat was now becoming dangerously familiar. It couldn't be Jacques! He lived and worked in a restaurant in Paris. He'd only been spending a few days down here in St Gabriel, doing his family a favour for a few days, on that fateful evening nearly five years ago. There had been a staff crisis in the local restaurant owned by his father, he'd told her, and Jacques had agreed to spend some of his holiday down here with the family.

But he'd told her he loved Paris and found the little town of St Gabriel too boring and sleepy. Nothing ever happened here. Jacques couldn't wait to get back to the bright lights of Paris and the exciting life he led there. He never came down here if he could help it.

Liz steeled herself to be strong as the memories came tumbling back. She'd always felt safe before when she'd visited her mother and sister. She'd been utterly convinced that she and Jacques would never meet again. They'd promised each other they would never ever make contact. Both had commitments and complicated lives that couldn't include each other. That idyllic night had been a once-in-a-lifetime experience....

Liz could feel her whole body stiffening with tension. She realised she was holding her breath as she watched the boat nearing the shore. She ought to be running the other way but, as if drawn by some magnetic force, she moved towards the sea, mesmerised by the swarthy, hunky figure of the man. Carrying both sandals in one hand, she flicked her long blonde hair behind her ears with the other. Was she unconsciously grooming herself in case it should be Jacques?

Don't be stupid! This man couldn't be Jacques! She was indulging herself in daydreams, in what might have been if only. And that was a silly thing to do, as she well knew from the amount of time she'd wasted in the still, small hours of the night, imagining what it would be like if she and Jacques had been free to...

She swallowed hard. She could see the basket of fish at the back of the boat, smell the scent of fresh fish, so different to the stuff that sometimes appeared on her plate in a restaurant. The man was standing in the stern of the small fishing boat, one bare brown foot casually gripping the wooden tiller with his toes as he steered the boat through the shallow water. He was making for the jetty. He slowed to wave to a child who was playing in the water near the shore, making absolutely sure that it was safe for him to tie up.

As the man leapt onto the jetty, the rope in one hand, pulling the boat in even as he leapt across the space, Liz gave an audible sigh of shock. The sound of the dying engine and the waves hitting the jetty covered up her fright. Yes, fright! Because that's what it was.

She'd never meant this to happen. Never in her wildest dreams had she conjured up the possibility that she would ever see Jacques again. Jacques belonged to that other life...even though he had every right to be an integral part in her new one. More than any other person in the world, he was the one who should, by rights, be with her now.

But that was impossible! For so many reasons, she must leave now…now…before he saw her.

Too late. The apparition had knotted the mooring rope and pulled himself up to his full height. He was staring across at her as she stood rooted to the spot, her hands clenching and unclenching as she held on to her sandals. One sandal fell onto the sand, then the other one. She didn't even notice. What did it matter? What did anything matter? Was it really Jacques, or a vision of her imagination brought on by being in the place where it had all started?

She stared hard at the vast expanse of bare, brown, black-haired chest, the salt-stained jeans clinging to the vision's muscular legs. Those legs that she remembered so well even five years on from that fateful night. She remembered tracing the firm muscular structure of his legs with her fingers during one mad moment, marvelling that a limb so firm and solid could induce such a sexy response in her.

Yes, it was Jacques, no doubt about it. His black hair was hanging down over his forehead, threatening to obscure his dark, ruggedly handsome face. He frowned, looking puzzled, no doubt as confused as she was.

But then he smiled, a wide, generous smile that seemed to emphasise his high cheekbones, the strong, jutting, darkly shadowed jaw.

'Elisabeth?'

He was running along the jetty now, calling her name, laughing out loud at the seeming absurdity of their meeting. She stood quite still. Her whole body felt paralysed with apprehension. Oh, yes, she longed to run towards him, throw herself into his arms…but she mustn't. No, no, she must remain calm, in charge of the situation.

Almost as if sensing her mood, Jacques slowed his

stride to a leisurely walking pace. He held both hands out towards her. She took hold of them, willing herself to stop trembling. If she held tight to his hands, kept her arms outstretched stiffly, she could make it quite clear that she didn't want him to kiss her. Oh, no, he mustn't kiss her. She was only flesh and blood after all, and any kind of close physical contact would break her resolve.

'Long time no see,' she said, in a voice that came out like a frog with a sore throat.

He was still smiling, displaying those dazzling white, strong, perfectly formed teeth.

Please, stop smiling, she wanted to say. Just turn around and pretend we've never met before. That would be the kindest way out of this impossible dilemma.

'*Qu'est-ce que tu fais ici*, Elisabeth? What are you doing here?'

At the sound of his voice, Liz felt her knees going weak. When they'd met before it had been his voice that had first attracted her. He'd smiled down at her in the restaurant as he'd helped her to decide what she wanted to eat, giving her the impression that he would continue to talk for hours about the fabulous food that was produced in his father's kitchen.

She'd been studying the menu, but at the sound of his voice she'd looked up and studied the man. There had been his physique, his sheer utter gorgeousness, if there was such a word. She hadn't been able to think of any other at the time, either in French or English. She'd never met a man like this before—or after. And the way he pronounced her name…Elisabeth. Only her French mother still called her by her full name, but Jacques—even though she'd only known him for a few hours—had insisted that it was too beautiful a name to be shortened.

He'd asked her what she was doing on the beach. His

dark eyes were searching her face as he waited for an answer.

'I could ask you the same question, Jacques.'

She realised they were still holding each other's hands and her arms were no longer stiff enough to hold Jacques away if he chose to kiss her. Quickly she pulled her hands away and dropped her eyes to look down at the wet sand, drawing a small circle with her big toe.

She cleared her throat. 'You're the last person I expected to see here. You said you couldn't stand St Gabriel. It was too boring and small a town. You preferred to stay in Paris.'

'Ah, Paris!' Jacques touched his fingers to his lips in a very Gallic gesture. 'Paris will always be my true love, but sometimes I like to escape from her. Like all lovers, she can become too demanding.'

Liz smiled. This was the Jacques she remembered. A man who didn't take anything seriously. During that fateful night he'd made her laugh more times than she could count. He didn't appear to live in the real world. His philosophy seemed to be that life was a huge joke. A huge, light-hearted adventure where you were meant to enjoy the moment, never thinking of what might follow. Today was all important. Tomorrow never came.

But tomorrow had come and she'd had to face the consequences, and life had moved on and they couldn't resume the nebulous charade they'd started that night. Real life required real people who took their responsibilities seriously.

Suddenly, the whole scene on the beach changed from poignant nostalgia to deadly serious action. Someone was screaming. A woman brushed passed Liz.

'*Au secours! Au secours!* Help! Somebody, please,

bring back my daughter. I can't see her any more and I can't swim.'

A crowd was gathering on the shore. Immediately, Jacques dropped his banter and took hold of the woman's arm.

'Show me where your daughter was swimming. Quickly, quickly! Point which way!'

'She was going over there beyond the jetty. Look, I can see her hand above the water.... Michèle! Michèle!'

The hand had disappeared beneath the water again, but Jacques was already hurtling through the waves, his strong muscular arms maintaining a furious, fast-paced crawl. A small crowd had gathered at the edge of the water, everyone noisily urging Jacques onward.

Liz watched as he reached the spot where the hand had appeared above the water. Now he was slowing down; he was diving beneath the surface. Seconds later he was resurfacing, gasping for air, only to plunge back into the depths again.

'Michèle!' the mother wailed. 'She's a good swimmer. She's only ten. But she has no fear of the water. She goes too far out. I keep telling her not to.... *Regardez! Le monsieur l'a trouvé.* He's found her! Michèle, oh, my poor baby...'

Liz held her breath as she watched Jacques resurfacing, this time holding what looked like a lifeless body. He was turning on to his back, the child's body on his chest as he cut back through the waves, his legs slicing furiously through the water.

The assembled crowd became silent as Jacques neared the shore. Liz realised from the grey appearance of the child's skin that most people had assumed that Michèle had been submerged too long to survive. As Jacques carried the child from the water, the mother rushed forward, once more screaming in anguish.

'She can't be dead. I know she's not dead. Call a doctor....'

Jacques put a steadying arm around the woman's shoulders. 'I am a doctor and I'm trained in lifesaving, *madame*. I will revive Michèle if I can.'

In the confusion of the moment, Liz wasn't sure she'd heard Jacques correctly, but the important thing was to resuscitate this poor child if that was possible.

She called to everybody to move out of the way as she knelt down on the wet sand next to the seemingly lifeless body. Jacques was panting heavily, desperately out of breath from his exertions in the water.

Liz checked Michèle for a pulse. No pulse. Neither was there any movement of the chest to indicate breathing.

'Let me help you, Jacques.' Liz put her arms across the body as Jacques turned the child on to her side.

A gush of foam-like froth emptied itself onto the sand.

'I'll clear her airway,' Liz said, placing a hand in the girl's throat.

Jacques gave her a puzzled glance as he struggled to catch his breath so he could continue with the resuscitation.

'It's OK. I'm trained in lifesaving,' she said briefly. 'Get your own breathing under control, Jacques, while I continue with the resuscitation.'

She bent down, closed the child's nostrils by pinching them with her thumb and index finger before sealing her lips over the young patient's mouth and blowing gently into her lungs, two slow full breaths with a pause in between, willing Michèle to breathe for herself. But the child's body seemed totally lifeless.

Jacques had regained control of his own breathing. He put a hand on Liz's shoulder. 'There's still no pulse. I'll begin chest compressions. We'll work together in sequence. You give two breaths, Elisabeth, and I'll follow with fifteen compressions.'

They repeated this sequence four times before checking Michèle's pulse again. Still no sign of life. Liz took a deep breath and bent over their patient's mouth once more. After several more sequences, Jacques called out that he could detect a faint pulse.

Liz rocked back on her heels. 'I can see a slight movement of the chest. Yes, Michèle's chest just moved again. She's breathing. Oh, Jacques, she's breathing by herself!'

There was a slight spluttering sound from the child. Jacques turned the girl onto her side as more water gushed from her mouth and then, miraculously, her eyes fluttered open and she stared around her.

'What happened? Where am I? Maman, Maman!'

'I'm here, *ma poupette*. Oh, Michèle!'

The mother's arms were around her child as she knelt down on the sand, crying with relief that her beloved daughter was still alive.

Liz looked across the tender, poignant scene of the mother reunited with her daughter and saw that Jacques was staring at her with an enigmatic expression in his eyes. For a few seconds they watched each other warily.

'Where did you learn your lifesaving, Elisabeth?'

'Where did you train as a doctor, Jacques? Are you a part-time doctor or a part-time waiter?'

He gave her a long slow smile. 'I'm a full-time doctor, but I used to help my father in his restaurant.'

He leaned forward to lift Michèle from the wet sand. 'I'm going to take our patient to hospital, *madame*,' he said to the child's mother. 'She will require further treatment in a place where we have all the necessary equipment. Come with me and…'

He broke off, looking down at Liz. 'And perhaps you would like to come to the hospital with us. You still haven't told me where you learned your lifesaving skills. Obviously…'

'I'm also a doctor,' Liz said quietly.

Jacques gave an exclamation of astonishment which was muffled by the sound of a siren wailing as an ambulance hurtled to the edge of the beach, skidding to a halt amid a pile of pebbles beneath the lime trees.

A couple of paramedics emerged with a stretcher and hurried to meet them.

'*Bonjour, Docteur Chenon*,' the first paramedic said, holding out his hands as if wanting to take charge of the young patient.

'*Bonjour, Frederick*,' Jacques said, still holding onto the child as he gently lowered her onto the stretcher before kneeling down to check that she was comfortable.

Bright, startled eyes were staring up at Jacques as the frightened patient clung to his hand.

'We're taking you to hospital, Michèle.'

'*Vous venez avec moi, monsieur?*' the child asked.

'Yes, I'm coming with you, *ma petite*,' Jacques said, smiling down at his patient. 'Don't look so worried. You're going to be fine.'

He stroked the tangled hair back from the child's forehead, smiling down at her and talking gently about how she was going to be treated when they got there. Liz watched the tender scene, marvelling at the revelation that this lovable rogue who had captured her heart in that one night of sheer madness was actually in the same caring profession as herself. She could see him already displaying a completely new and very surprising side to his character.

In the ambulance, Liz sat next to Michèle's mother, helping to calm her and assuring her that her daughter was going to make a full recovery. Jacques fixed a cannula into Michèle's arm and attached it to an intravenous infusion of glucose and saline. The child was obviously in a state of shock and she needed fluids to help her recovery. He'd checked her blood pressure, which was too low but not dangerously so. Her breathing needed to be stabilised.

'Breathe into this mask, Michèle,' he told his patient, placing the oxygen mask over her face. 'That's a good girl. Nice deep breaths, slow and steady…'

Michèle's mother had closed her eyes and was swaying to the movement of the ambulance.

Jacques glanced at Elisabeth. During that heady, exciting night they'd spent together he'd never imagined she was a doctor. Why had she told him she didn't work, that she was just a housewife, content to stay at home? A little white lie perhaps so that he wouldn't be able to trace her again? Or had she, too, felt the need to be someone else that night, as he had when he'd told her he always worked as a waiter?

He leaned forward so that he could speak quietly to her. As he did so, he caught a whiff of her perfume, that hauntingly evocative scent that had driven him wild on that first and only time he'd met her.

Mon dieu, she was beautiful! She hadn't changed. She'd appeared in his father's restaurant like a vision from another world and he'd known that he'd been drawn to her in a way that had never happened to him before. She was looking at him in surprise, wondering why he was hovering so close to her. He had to find out more, find out everything that had happened to her in the five years since their wonderful night together....

'Where are you working now, Elisabeth?'

'I...I've just changed jobs. I finished working in a hospital in London last week. Tomorrow I start work at the Clinique de la Côte.'

Jacques was startled. 'In St Gabriel?'

Liz smiled. 'Well, how many Cliniques de la Côte are there along this stretch of the Mediterranean coast? Do you know the Clinique?'

'That's where I work,' Jacques said quietly.

Liz looked at him, her eyes wide with surprise as her body churned with the emotions thrown up by the realisation that they would have to work together.

'Oh, I see.' She felt shell-shocked. She couldn't think of anything else to say.

Jacques smiled. 'Yes, I know what you're thinking.'

To her annoyance, a slow blush spread across her cheeks.

'I very much doubt it.'

'You're thinking that we'll find it impossibly hard to work together, aren't you, Elisabeth?'

'Put it this way, it will be a challenge, but I'll manage somehow—I hope.'

As if to make the point, Liz bent down to examine their patient more closely. 'Michèle's breathing is more stable. Shall we try her without the oxygen mask, Dr Chenon?'

Jacques nodded, a serious expression on his face. 'I think that would be a good idea, Dr Elisabeth.'

They both smiled at the pseudo-formality they were trying to achieve, each of them desperate to form some kind of professional rapport out of the unusual beginning to their relationship. Their hands touched as Liz removed the mask from the patient's face. She felt a spark of awareness running through her. No, it wasn't going to be easy maintaining a professional stance with Jacques, but that's what she must do.

Jacques had been a couple of weeks away from his wedding when she'd last seen him. He would have been married almost five years now. She always kept married men at arm's length. They were a no-go area in her book. She wasn't even going to allow herself to dream about what might have been, and that was all the more reason now why her own situation must remain a secret.

'We're arriving at the hospital,' Jacques said. 'I hadn't realised that you were actually going to be on the staff here when I asked you to come with me. You don't start work until tomorrow so if you prefer to—'

'No, I'd like to come with you,' Liz said quickly, as she moved the oxygen cylinder to one side so that the paramedics could reach around to the back of Michèle's stretcher.

The doors of the ambulance were now wide open. Liz remained at Michèle's side as the stretcher was lifted out onto the forecourt of the clinic. Liz looked up at the clean white stones of the new building and above that to the cloudless blue sky. So different to the grimy grey stone of the hospital topped by a seemingly endless blanket of cloud where she'd been working in London.

She thought she'd changed her life around by coming out here to St Gabriel. All she'd done had been to exchange one set of problems for an infinitely more complex situation. But she didn't want to go back to the way things had been.

Michèle was taken away to a treatment room as soon as they went into the hospital. Liz promised the young girl she would find time to go and see her the next day when she was on duty. Jacques had said that Michèle would be kept in for two days' observation until her condition had stabilised. It had been made quite obvious that Michèle was no longer her patient and Liz decided that the best thing she could do was leave the hospital staff to take care of her.

Jacques had gone off somewhere to make an accident report and she hadn't seen him for some time. She moved down the corridor and made for the front door, stepping to one side as a porter and a nurse passed her with a stretcher bearing an unconscious patient coming back from the operating theatre.

Halfway out of the wide open door she heard someone calling her name.

'Dr Elisabeth!'

She felt a frisson of excitement as she recognised the voice.

'I'm so glad I caught you.' Jacques sounded out of breath. 'I hurried down the corridor. I'd just had to check on that patient who passed you in the corridor. One of my junior registrars had been working on the case in Theatre and my senior registrar wanted me to make sure all was well before we let the patient go back to the ward.'

'Are you a surgeon?'

'Yes. I…I'm head of surgery here.' He smiled. 'More interesting than waiting on tables.'

She looked up at Jacques. People were milling around them like busy little ants in a colony, carrying things, moving things. For a few moments she felt as if she'd been transported back to London.

Jacques put a hand under her arm. 'Let's get out of here. Neither of us is officially on duty so…'

'Jacques, there's something I must tell you,' she began,

but Jacques was still propelling her forward. She tried to keep up the pace with him until they were well clear of the front of the hospital.

'I know a quiet little bar on the seafront where we can—'

'Jacques, I ought to be going home.'

He stopped dead in his tracks and the expression on his face changed. 'To your husband?'

'No, no. I divorced Mike. I—'

'*Eh bien!*' Jacques said softly, sympathetically. 'You did the right thing. So, why don't we go and celebrate?'

She took a deep breath. His enthusiasm for life was infectious—just as it had been five years ago. Such hidden power in his voice when he spoke. Finding that he wasn't a roguish, footloose and fancy-free waiter didn't make any difference. There was a magnetic force that simply drew her towards him. Yes, he was charismatic, but that didn't explain how she found it so hard to resist him.

'We'll have one drink—for old times' sake,' she added quickly. 'And then I have to go home. My...'

She paused. She couldn't even speak her darling daughter's name in front of Jacques. She knew she would blush, falter, give the show away.... And Jacques mustn't know. He must never know her impossible secret.

She began again. 'My mother and sister will be wondering where I am. I only went down to the beach for a short walk.'

Jacques slowed his pace and turned towards her, placing one long, sensitive finger under her chin.

'Elisabeth,' he drawled in that furiously unnervingly attractive accent that sent shivers of excitement running down her spine.

The sound of his voice was so melodious to Liz's ears.

How many times had she lain awake, wishing she could hear him speak again? Even contemplating, wickedly, about trying to find out his phone number so that she could hear his voice, possibly on his answering machine. But then she'd come to her senses, told herself it was a stupid, teenage thing to do and would only open up old wounds that were healing nicely…well, healing over slowly.

And here she was with the vision actually in the flesh, about to spend every day working in the same hospital as him. It was just too incredible for words—and too vastly unworkable!

One drink, she told herself firmly as Jacques propelled her to a seat outside a beach-side bar. He waited until she was seated before drawing up a wooden chair next to her and leaning across the table to adjust the angle of the huge, multicoloured parasol.

'There, that's better,' Jacques said. 'The sun is moving in that direction. It sets over the other side of the cliff so we'll have good shade for—'

'Jacques, we're only staying for one drink.'

He smiled. 'You may have one drink, Dr Elisabeth, but I shall have at least two. First I need an enormous bottle of water. I think I swallowed too much sea water while I was trying to find Michèle and my throat feels salty.'

Liz nodded. 'I'm very thirsty, too.'

A waiter was hovering by their table. Jacques ordered a large bottle of water and two glasses. 'And what would you like besides water, Elisabeth?'

'I'd like a *crème de cassis* with white wine, my favourite drink when I'm in France.'

'*Un kir*,' Jacques told the waiter.

For a few moments they remained silent, each of them

studying the other. Jacques was unable to believe his good fortune in meeting up with the woman who'd constantly been in his thoughts for the past five years. He'd assumed she would have stayed with her rat of a husband.

Liz was unable to believe that she was actually here with the man she'd tried to forget without success. But in her case she was constantly reminded on a daily basis about this man. His existence was always patently obvious in her own family situation.

'So, you had the courage to get rid of him, then,' Jacques said, leaning towards her, unable to disguise his admiration.

Liz hesitated. 'I thought long and hard about what I should do. Mike and I had been married since we were medical students and it wasn't easy to break up the marriage.'

'Elisabeth, you didn't break up the marriage. It was your husband who did that when he…how do you say it in English? He two-timed you, *n'est-ce pas*?'

Liz nodded, feeling the rush of unhappiness that always accompanied this revelation. She'd long since stopped loving Mike but it still hurt, the fact that he'd deceived her like that.

'Yes, Mike was the one who started having affairs. I think I could have forgiven one affair, but when another of my so-called friends and colleagues confessed that she'd had an affair with Mike only a couple of months after we were married, I realised I was living with a serial philanderer. Mike was insatiable where women were concerned and this sort of thing was going to bc a constant feature of our marriage. Either I turned a blind eye or I made a clean break.'

'But you weren't sure what you were going to do when I last saw you.'

'Not when I first came out here, but…' She hesitated. 'I think I came to a decision soon afterwards.'

She leaned back in her chair, looking up at the gaudy parasol, feeling the warmth of the late afternoon sun beating through it. Oh, yes, she'd made her decision at the end of that wonderful night she'd spent with Jacques. She'd realised that she'd lost all love and respect for Mike after what he'd done to her and she knew, without a shadow of a doubt, that their love for each other had been flawed in the first place.

They'd been teenage sweethearts in medical school, seeing each other every day. It had been the first time Liz had known the power of sex and it had seemed the ideal solution to move in with each other. It had been only one step further to get married and that, to twenty-year-old Liz had seemed like a dream. Only when the reality of the situation had set in had she seen what a mistake she'd made.

'How soon after our night together did you make your decision?' His eyes were searching her face.

She took a large gulp of water, followed by a tentative sip of her kir. The strong blackcurrant taste soothed the back of her throat and calmed her, as it always did. She remembered her sister giving her a kir on the day their father had died.

Liz put down her glass and raised her eyes once more to look at Jacques.

'I realised that I was as guilty as Mike by allowing myself to make love with you that night,' she said in a half-whisper. 'Just because my husband had been unfaithful, that didn't give me the right to follow his example, but…'

Her voice faltered. She knew she couldn't go on without making a complete fool of herself, but there were things that had to be said.

Jacques had risen to his feet and was leaning over her, his arms around her shoulders, holding her, oh, so tightly, so comfortingly, so disturbingly.

'I know how you felt, Elisabeth, because I too felt guilty that I'd… Well, it wasn't the sort of thing I'd ever done before, taken a beautiful woman out for the first time and practically seduced her so that… Look, let's walk on the sand where we can talk more freely.'

Jacques tossed some money on to the table, one arm still around Liz's shoulder, drawing her to her feet. They walked across the small terrace out onto the sandy path that led to the sea.

The tide was in, lapping against the shore. Jacques shielded his eyes from the sun and stared along to the end of the long curved beach. In the distance, below the cliff, he could just make out the jetty where he'd abandoned his boat and the precious catch from his off-duty afternoon's fishing.

'I'll have to go and bring my boat back to St Gabriel harbour this evening,' Jacques said. 'Do you want to come with me? We could have supper on the boat. I'm going to grill fresh fish, straight from the sea and—'

'I can't, Jacques.' She turned to look at him. 'My family… I have to get back. I've stayed too long already. But you… What about your wife?'

'My wife? Oh, you mean Francine.' He raised his eyebrows. 'I remember it was only two weeks before we were due to be married, wasn't it?'

He ran his tongue around his lips. 'I phoned Francine in Paris the next day to tell her I couldn't go through with the wedding. Then I asked my *témoin*—that's the French equivalent of the best man—to cancel everything.

I believe I told you I'd been wondering whether to call off the wedding. My relationship with my fiancée had been getting worse. Meeting you that night made me realise the honest course of action I had to take.'

Liz ran a hand through her long hair, unconsciously removing one of the tangles.

'So, at the very least, our night together helped us to make some important decisions.'

Jacques looked out at the blue sea and the tiny flecks of foam on the waves near the shore. For a brief moment he was transported back in time to that soul-restoring night with Elisabeth.

'You know, Elisabeth,' he said, slowly, 'when I came down from Paris the day before I met you, I was feeling emotionally bruised and battered. Francine and I had been living together for two years. We'd both agreed we didn't want marriage and family. We simply wanted to enjoy ourselves and make the most of our life in Paris. I worked hard at the hospital, Francine had her modelling career and—'

'So why did you decide to marry?' Liz said, intrigued by the husky, emotional tone of his voice.

Jacques looked down at her with troubled eyes. 'Francine had said she didn't want to marry but then she changed her mind. I went along with it at first, but in the final weeks before the wedding I started having serious doubts. We were quarrelling about it all the time we were together.'

He drew in his breath, knowing he'd explained as much as he could. He wasn't going to tell Elisabeth why he'd allowed Francine to live with him in the first place. Ever since he'd suffered that disastrous bout of mumps when he'd been a medical student, ever since he'd gone through the trauma of being diagnosed as sterile, he'd avoided relationships with girls who wanted a permanent commitment. But Francine had professed to be different. She didn't want a permanent relationship, she'd said, and then she'd changed her mind.

In his mind's eye he had a sudden flashback to that dreadful day when Marcel, the doctor who'd looked after him during his illness, had given him the life-shattering news that he could never be a father. Mumps at age twenty was a very dangerous illness, Marcel had told him. Jacques could feel the horror of the revelation even now.

He remembered quite clearly how Marcel had put an arm round his shoulders and tried to comfort him before offering advice. He'd said that Jacques could choose to take one of two courses of action. He could either go home to his family for a long period of convalescence, tell them the sad news of his sterility and wallow in their pity, or he could keep silent, get on with his medical studies, concentrate on his career and build up a full life.

Thinking about the devastating effect the news of his sterility would have on his child-loving family, he hadn't hesitated in his choice of getting straight back in the saddle at the hospital and adopting his current way of life where his life was so full that there wasn't time to dwell on the fact that he would never be a father.

Francine was the only person he'd told about his sterility and that had been simply because she'd been angling to move into his apartment. He'd had to tell her the truth, that if she was thinking about a permanent relationship it wasn't a good idea because he wouldn't be able to father children. She'd seemed relieved, had told him she didn't want children and he'd believed her.

But later, after Francine had talked him into the idea of marriage, she'd begun to taunt him about his sterility, one minute saying it didn't matter, the next saying that she might like children in the future but she was prepared to tolerate a childless marriage if that was all he could offer. During one particularly acrimonious argument with Francine he'd realised it had been a terrible mistake to go into their relationship in the first place. Francine had pointed out that he couldn't offer her or any woman a real future. He wouldn't make that mistake again.

So he knew he couldn't tell Elisabeth the whole story and he certainly couldn't get too involved with her. He couldn't tell her that Francine had known he was sterile but that hadn't worried her when she'd first moved in. She'd said she didn't want children. As a model she'd wanted to look after her figure. But little by little she'd changed, she'd subtly worn him down with repeated talk about marriage.

He'd suspected that if they did marry, as Francine grew older and her modelling career was waning, she might decide she definitely wanted children after all. She would resent the fact that he couldn't give her a family and he would be torn apart at being unable to become a father. As Francine had pointed out so viciously, he couldn't give any woman a real future.

Even before Francine had said this, he'd known in his heart of hearts that he didn't want to go through with a childless marriage. He desperately wanted children of his own, but that wasn't possible and he'd learned to live with it. He was totally committed to his medical career but in his private life he'd learned to pretend that he was a carefree bachelor type who enjoyed the good things in life and avoided commitment to a permanent relationship.

Taking Marcel's advice had been the only way of coping with the trauma of his medical condition. Deep down he could feel the aching agony of knowing he would never have a child. Yes, he'd learned to cope with it. But no woman should have to suffer because he couldn't give her the family she craved.

'Jacques, are you all right?'

Elisabeth was looking up at him with an anxious expression on her face.

He gave her a reassuring smile. Got to keep up the pretence.

'I'm fine! I was remembering what a good thing it was that I cancelled the wedding. I'm just not the marrying kind—it's as simple as that. I prefer my freedom. Marriage and children would change all that.'

He looked down at Elisabeth's lovely face. He'd made it quite clear now exactly how he felt about a committed relationship, but it still hurt him to think that he couldn't hope for a future with her. He could only hope for a light-hearted romance where neither of them would get hurt. Especially Elisabeth. He was tough and had learned to take whatever life threw at him, but he must never hurt this tender creature.

She was looking so beautiful in the slanting rays of the early evening sunlight. On impulse, he bent his head and touched her lips lightly with his own.

At the feel of his sexy, sensual mouth on hers, Liz felt a shiver of anticipation. This was how it had all started, that night on the beach. But it mustn't happen again! She had to make it perfectly clear to Jacques that—

But he was already pulling away, looking down at her with a serious expression in his eyes.

'Yes, our night together changed everything for me,' he said solemnly.

Liz turned away. Her heart was thumping madly. Jacques had no idea just how much her *own* life had been changed.

CHAPTER TWO

'HI, EVERYBODY, I'm home!'

Liz closed the solid oak door behind her and hurried along the terracotta tiles of the hall to the old farmhouse-style kitchen. Her sister Gina turned round from the cooker, the large spoon in her slender hand still dripping into the cassoulet she was cooking, and smiled. Two years older than Liz, Gina's hair was blonde like Liz's, but she wore it slightly shorter although still touching the shoulders. They were often taken for twins but their close friends could see many subtle differences in their appearance and major differences in personality.

Liz had wanted to be a doctor since spending a few weeks in hospital as a child, so she'd always worked hard to pass her exams. Gina loved needlework and cooking but hated academic work. She'd always wanted to work with children, so she'd made a great effort to scrape through the necessary exams. Married at the age of twenty-one, she'd worked as a primary school teacher for a couple of years before leaving so that she could spend more time at home, helping her husband with his struggling career as a writer.

Gina gave her sister a welcoming smile. 'Had a good walk?'

'You could say that.' Liz sank down on to a chair at the huge wooden kitchen table. 'Where's Melissa?'

'Mum took her to see Sidonie soon after you went out. It's Sidonie's birthday. Mum had forgotten she'd promised to take Melissa so that she could show off her granddaughter to some friends. I expect they're still gorging themselves on birthday cake. Would you like a drink?'

'I've just had one—well, at least I started to drink it but then we went for a walk and— Oh, Gina, I met Jacques again.'

'Oh, lord! You didn't. Did you tell him about—?'

'Of course I didn't. We always said—'

'Good.' Gina bent down to put the cassoulet in the oven, before reaching into the fridge for a bottle of wine. 'I think we need to talk before Mum gets back with Melissa.'

Liz reached for a corkscrew and uncorked the wine while Gina found a couple of glasses. Liz raised her glass towards her sister.

'I can't believe he's actually living here in St Gabriel. Not after he'd said he couldn't stand the place and—'

'Is he still working for his father at the restaurant?'

'You're never going to believe this! Jacques isn't really a waiter. He's a doctor.'

Gina's eyes widened and she took a large gulp of wine. 'You're right. I don't believe it. You're sure he's not having you on? Making it all up? He sounded like a very dodgy character to me.'

Liz banged her glass down on the table and glared indignantly at her sister. 'Gina, Jacques is not a dodgy character! I said he'd told me he didn't want to be tied down, he liked the bright lights of Paris, having a wild time, lots of travel and—'

'And you also said he told you he didn't want a family, Liz.'

Liz frowned. 'That doesn't make him a dodgy character. He's simply different to your average run-of-the-mill man.'

She took a sip of wine as she remembered her conversation with Jacques that evening. He'd told her again that he didn't want a family and all the responsibility it involved. Made it quite obvious he wasn't into committed relationships. She groaned inwardly. Jacques hadn't changed his ideas about freedom and independence in the past five years.

'Yes, Jacques implied he still likes having a good time and doesn't want to take on responsibilities,' Liz told Gina quietly. 'Maybe it's because he works hard at the hospital so when he's off duty he likes to enjoy himself. No harm in that.... Gina, he really is a doctor! There was a young girl who nearly drowned down on the beach and Jacques and I resuscitated her, after which we took her to the hospital.'

'To the Clinique de la Côte?'

'Where else? It's the best hospital for miles around here. And everybody knows Jacques because he's head of surgery there. That's how responsible he is.'

'But not responsible enough to want children of his own.'

Liz stood up, still clutching her wineglass as she walked over to the kitchen window. The garden looked so peaceful. She felt the urge to walk out there and leave this discussion, but she knew that with Gina, her only confidante in the dilemma of her single motherhood, she had to set the record straight.

'Lots of people don't want children nowadays. When I met Jacques five years ago he told me that he'd been living with his fiancée Francine for a couple of years and they'd both agreed that children didn't fit in with their free and easy lifestyle.'

'Is Francine still with him?' Gina reached across the table and topped up Liz's glass.

'Jacques cancelled the wedding. He said he couldn't go through with it.'

'Wow!' Gina whistled softly. 'That must have been some night you two spent together. I remember you next day, in a state of starry-eyed uselessness, weeping one minute because you'd agreed not to see Jacques again, then planning to divorce Mike. Mum didn't know why the two of us had to keep going out into the garden and—'

'Gina, promise me you won't tell Mum.'

'As if I would! Look, we've kept the secret ever since you first told me you were pregnant. Mum's always assumed Mike was Melissa's father. Well, you were still married when you became pregnant.'

Liz nodded. 'And the fact that our divorce had come through by the time Melissa was born didn't seem to worry Mum.'

'Mum never liked Mike,' Gina said. 'I think she was relieved he'd gone off to Australia with his latest girlfriend and had asked not to be contacted except through his solicitor. He didn't even know you were pregnant. Well, that was how it seemed to me.'

'And me,' Liz said. 'Anyway, Mike made it perfectly clear that he wasn't remotely interested in what I did with the rest of my life.'

'So, we're agreed, aren't we?' Gina said. 'Mum doesn't know anything and that's the way it's got to stay. She's had one heart attack. Even with her medication her blood pressure rises dangerously high when she gets upset. Heaven knows what would happen if she thought her darling granddaughter was the result of a one-night stand.'

'Gina, it wasn't like that!'

'So what was it like? No, don't tell me. I can imagine,

from what you've already said. Jacques was the love of your life. A once-in-a-lifetime experience. But are you going to tell him about Melissa? A man who probably wouldn't want to accept paternity anyway, given that he says he doesn't want a family. A man who still doesn't want the responsibility of a child?'

'I've no intention of telling Jacques,' Liz said quietly. 'I couldn't tell him before even if I'd wanted to because, firstly, I thought he'd be married, secondly, we'd promised never to contact each other again, thirdly, I felt so guilty as a still married woman that I'd allowed myself to make love with someone I'd only known a few hours. Someone who was due to get married himself in a couple of weeks and—'

'Ssh, that's Mum and Melissa. Here, wipe your eyes, they're all runny.'

Liz moved back to the table. Gina handed Liz a tissue.

Liz flashed Gina a grateful smile as she dabbed at her eyes. 'Thanks, Gina, for being so supportive.'

Gina gave her sister a quick hug. 'That's what big sisters are for.'

There was the sound of footsteps on the tiles in the hall. The door opened and a little girl with long dark hair, done up with a red ribbon in a becoming ponytail, burst into the kitchen.

'Maman, Maman!' Melissa threw her arms around her mother's neck.

Liz nuzzled her face into the scented hair and thought how lucky she was to have such a wonderful daughter. Yes, Melissa had been a mistake, but the most wonderful mistake of her life. She couldn't imagine life without her.

Melissa was now scrambling onto her lap, talking in rapid French about the party they'd been to. Melissa usually talked in French when she'd been out with

Grandmaman Karine, but if she was alone with Liz or Gina they usually spoke English. Liz had encouraged her daughter to speak both languages from the time she'd said her first words, and they'd spent as much time as they could here in France before actually moving here.

Melissa didn't seem to notice which language she was speaking. Switching between the two was perfectly natural to her, as it had been with Liz when she'd talked to her English father and French mother.

'There were all these old ladies eating cake and drinking wine,' Melissa was explaining with solemn, childish directness as she mimicked the way the ladies had looked.

Karine gave a tinkling laugh and ran a hand over her chic, expensively cut, highlighted blonde hair.

'Please, Melissa, don't call me old.'

Melissa grinned. 'I didn't mean you, Grandmaman, but some of your friends are really…well, sort of ancient. They creak and groan when they stand up. Sidonie only had one candle on her cake so I think she must be a hundred.'

Karine chuckled. *'Que tu es méchante, Melissa!'*

'But I like her a lot. I like all your friends, Grandmaman,' the little girl said quickly, aware that she might have said something naughty but not knowing what it had been.

'I'd love to be as old as they are and have lots of sparkling brooches and big diamond rings and dangly pearls from my ears. Can I have my ears pierced when I'm four and a half, Maman? I'm four and a quarter now, but in three months' time…'

'Of course you can, darling,' Grandmaman Karine said, answering for her daughter.

Liz gave an inaudible sigh as she looked across the

table at Gina. Whatever Melissa wanted, she could have, according to their doting mother. Melissa was in danger of becoming spoilt. But Liz knew she mustn't be ungrateful to be living in this warm family ambience.

She'd tried the independent lifestyle of single mother, taking her daughter to a London nursery each morning, picking her up in the evening and taking her back to a lonely flat in a high-rise block. That hadn't been good for either of them. So whenever she felt irritated by not being able to have full control over Melissa, she reminded herself of all the benefits and counted her blessings.

They'd only been living here for a week but already Melissa was adapting to her new life. She loved the rambling old house, the large garden, with its swing, fish pond, paddling pool and sandpit. It was the perfect place to bring up a child. In fact, the lifestyle couldn't be better. Apart from the fact that Melissa didn't have a father like the other friends she would meet when Liz enrolled her at the *école maternelle*, the local nursery school.

But you couldn't have everything in this life. And Melissa hadn't seemed to suffer so far from being brought up without a father. Liz had made sure of that.

'Cassoulet for supper, Maman,' Gina said, lifting the huge dish from the oven.

'Oh, darling, I'm only going to eat salad tonight,' Karine told her daughter. '*Il faut garder la ligne!* I have to keep my figure!'

Karine placed her hands on her waist, trying to pull in the slim contours of her beautifully tailored grey suit even further.

'I was forced to eat some of Sidonie's cake just to be polite,' Karine continued. 'So I'll compensate for that by missing your delicious cassoulet, Gina, if you don't mind.'

Karine smiled as she watched her daughters and granddaughter. 'But Liz must have some cassoulet. She's become too thin since she's been working in London. They don't eat properly over there. I remember when I was a student working as an au pair. No lunch—well, a cheese sandwich or something. That's not lunch. I was permanently hungry. One of the reasons I started going out with your father was because he was rich enough to buy me a proper lunch.'

Liz smiled at Gina over the top of Melissa's head as she lifted her from her lap so that she could start setting the table. They'd both heard the story of the whirlwind romance so often. Young homesick French girl meets older, richer, handsome English university professor while taking English lessons.

'Is that Grandpapa you're talking about, Grandmaman?' Melissa asked, picking up the photograph of a smiling, crinkly-eyed, distinguished-looking man from one of the bookshelves at one end of the kitchen and transferring herself to Karine's lap.

'Tell me some more about how he was teaching you to speak English and then he asked you if you'd like to go for a walk by the river in London. Was it that big river Mummy and I used to live near? Can't remember its name.'

'The Thames, darling,' Karine said, settling her granddaughter on her lap. 'Well, you see, one day when…'

'Where's Clive?' Liz asked her sister, quietly so as not to disturb the true love story that was intriguing her daughter just as she had been intrigued by it at around the same age. 'Will he be in for supper?'

Gina explained that her husband was out at a literary

meeting in the next town and wouldn't be back until much later. 'I'll save a bowl of cassoulet and some salad for him. He loves going to these meetings where he meets other writers who're having a hard time like himself. I just hope somebody wants to publish the book he's working on. He hasn't been in print since that first book five years ago and he's beginning to think it was just a flash in the pan.'

'Oh, he'll get into print again,' Liz said. 'I think he's got real talent.'

'Do you?' Gina looked up, her face flushed from her exertions at the cooker. 'It's good to be reassured when you're having doubts, Liz.'

'Well, you always help to reassure me when I have my own doubts.'

Liz swallowed the lump in her throat as she thought about all the times her sister had helped her during the last five years.

'Come on, let's serve up.'

She turned to look at her daughter who was now stroking Mimi, their black and white cat.

'Come and wash your hands, darling. And then, as soon as you've finished supper, I'll take you up to bed.'

Melissa gave Mimi a final stroke. 'Will you read that story about the cat that got lost in the forest and a little girl found it and took it home and—?'

'Yes, of course I will.'

As she helped her daughter to dry her hands on the kitchen towel Liz was thinking how good it was to have some family life to take her mind off the fact that she was starting a new job tomorrow.

Yes, she was working in a new hospital tomorrow...but that was the least of her worries.

* * *

Liz was feeling very much the new girl as she went nervously through the front entrance of the hospital. Yesterday had been different. She hadn't been officially on duty. But today she had to make her mark. Show the rest of her colleagues that she could actually do her job.

'Excusez-moi, madame, mais est-ce que vous êtes le docteur Fitzgerald?'

Liz smiled gratefully at the young nurse in the white uniform who had been waiting inside the door. Somebody actually knew who she was!

'Yes, I'm Dr Fitzgerald.'

'I've been asked to take you to see our head of surgery. Dr Chenon would like to explain your duties, I believe, Dr Fitzgerald.'

'Thank you, Nurse…?'

'I'm Béatrice.'

'I'm Liz. It's short for Elisabeth.'

The nurse smiled. 'Leez…so very English!' She stopped in front of a door at the end of the corridor.

'This is the office of Dr Chenon. See you later, Dr Liz. *À tout à l'heure!*'

Jacques rose to his feet and came round the desk, crossing the carpeted room with easy strides.

'Elisabeth.' He took hold of both her hands.

For one heady moment she thought he was going to kiss her. She stiffened with something akin to fear. She mustn't give in to this treacherous feeling that she wanted Jacques to take her in his arms. The moment passed as Jacques turned and went back behind his desk. She'd simply imagined there was a current of passion running between them. They were both here to work.

'Do, please, sit down, Elisabeth,' Jacques said, smiling as he indicated a chair in front of his desk.

'As you were probably told at your interview in

London, our hospital is due to expand a great deal in the near future, but for the present we have to make sure that each department is covered by enough staff who are not necessarily specialists but who have had training and experience in that particular medical area.'

He paused for a moment, looking directly at her, an enigmatic expression on his face. Liz waited for him to continue. Perhaps he was checking that she could follow his rapid French.

'You don't have to worry about me understanding what you say,' she interjected.

Jacques smiled. 'No, I wasn't worried about that. You told me you had a French mother and that you'd lived in France.'

He leaned forward, his eyes searching her face. She wondered why he didn't continue.

Jacques took a deep breath. *Mon dieu*, this was so difficult, trying to be professional with the woman who'd affected him more than anyone else had ever done! He'd only known her a few hours but she'd captured his heart completely. He hadn't tried to contact her in the intervening years because they'd promised each other they wouldn't. And anyway he'd had the impression she would probably soldier on with her ailing marriage. She'd seemed the sort of girl who would stick things out to the bitter end, regardless of her own feelings, if she felt it was her duty to do so.

But now here she was, like the answer to his prayers, and he had no idea how to handle the situation because, instead of relishing her freedom from the tyranny of her dreadful marriage, she was definitely putting up a barrier between them. There had to be something she wasn't telling him.

Perhaps there was someone else in her life. Some important person who now shared her life and demanded she be totally faithful to him. He had to find out.

'As I was saying, the Clinique de la Côte is in a period of transition,' Jacques continued in his most professional voice. 'As head of surgery, I've been asked to take charge of a number of departments. I understand, Elisabeth, that you were working in Accident and Emergency in your London hospital.'

Liz nodded. 'Yes, I was.' She felt relieved that Jacques had stopped scrutinising her in that unnerving way. She was almost beginning to wonder if a mistake had been made in her appointment as a doctor here. Or was Jacques wondering if it would be a mistake for her to work in the same hospital as him?

'But you have also had considerable experience in surgery, I believe.'

Jacques glanced up from the notes he'd been scanning.

'Yes, I was training in general surgery when I switched to A and E.'

'*Pourquoi?* Why was that?'

Liz took a deep breath. 'It seemed the logical career move to make at the time. There were problems in my personal life and I didn't think at the time that I had enough physical strength to commit to several more years of strenuous…' She broke off. 'Look, what is this, Jacques? This is more like a job interview than a work briefing. Why are you asking me all these questions? Just tell me what my duties are and…'

Jacques rose from his seat and came round to Liz's side of the desk. He pulled up a chair next to her and leaned across to place his fingers lightly on either side of her cheeks in a decidedly unprofessional manner.

'It's because I care about you that I want to be sure you'll be happy here,' he said gently.

Some inner demon led her to bring her hands up and place them over his. Oh, the touch of his skin against hers! What rapturous memories it evoked. She knew full well she shouldn't be doing this but she simply couldn't help herself.

'I know I'm going to be happy here, Jacques,' she said quietly, before removing her hands as she came to her senses again. Carefully, she began to get up from her chair. 'I'd like to go and do some work now.'

Jacques pulled himself to his full height and took a step backwards so that they were facing each other with a few paces between them. He'd got the message. Work was important to Elisabeth and she didn't want to mix work with pleasure.

'Because of your past experience in these areas, we're placing you in A and E initially. But you must know that our A and E staff also take clinics in Outpatients on certain days. There is an amalgamation between the two departments which works very well as we're still a small hospital. Over the next few years this will be phased out. And you may also be asked to use your surgical skills on occasion, if you agree.'

Liz looked up at Jacques and felt that indescribable tingle of excitement which rushed through her when she was anywhere near him. She felt at this moment that she would agree to anything if it meant she could spend time with him in a not-too-compromising situation. So long as she could hold on to her emotions and not get carried away, it would be wonderful to work alongside the man who had given her a daughter. Melissa was the most precious gift of her life.

'Yes, I would enjoy working in surgery again.'

A pang of regret shot through her. If only she could share the wonderful news that they had a child between them. But reluctantly she admitted that Jacques would be horrified for all the reasons she'd worried about for so long. He'd made it quite clear he didn't want children back then, and nothing he said or did now indicated any change of heart.

She remembered one of her male colleagues in London who'd been confronted by a woman who'd claimed he was the father of her child. He'd fought tooth and nail to deny it, even going as far as DNA testing. When it was proved he actually was the father, he'd shouldered his responsibilities from a financial point of view but, as far as Liz knew, he'd never even seen the child.

And he shunned all contact with the mother of his child. Oh, no, she wasn't going to go through that! She had to cling to her secret and try to maintain a platonic relationship. But it wasn't going to be easy.

'They're expecting you in A and E this morning.'

'Fine!' She began to move towards the door but Jacques put his hand on her arm to detain her.

'Just one more question.' He paused, before clearing his throat. 'Will you have dinner with me tonight, Elisabeth?'

She looked up into his eyes and was amazed to see an expression which was almost pleading. From a handsome, obviously much sought-after man, this was very flattering for her. She should resist, but the short interview with Jacques had already weakened her resolve. If Gina wasn't going out tonight and could babysit, she'd take Jacques up on his offer.

She smiled. 'Who was it once said they could resist anything except temptation?'

Jacques laughed. 'Oscar Wilde perhaps. But why do you regard having dinner with me as temptation? If I promise not to take you on the beach and seduce you as I did last time, will you come?'

She pushed her hair behind her ears and moved towards him. 'I wouldn't exactly say you seduced me. It was a mutual understanding that we both needed each other that night. We'd both suffered. We were both trying to decide how we were going to deal with our disastrous relationships and...well, in my case anyway, I couldn't stop myself from making love with you.'

He reached down and drew her into the circle of his arms. Liz could feel the hardness of his muscular chest beneath the soft texture of his suit jacket. She tried not to press against him but knew that some unseen force was rendering her incapable of holding off. When his lips came down on hers she sighed with rapturous abandon just as she had done five years ago. But something deep inside her was telling her that she mustn't go down that road again.

'No, Jacques. Not here!'

He looked down at her with a rakish smile as she pulled away. He knew he was playing with fire when all he could offer was a light romance, but he couldn't help himself. And Elisabeth seemed to be enjoying his flirtatious advances.

'Does that mean I can hope you'll find it hard to resist me if we're in a more suitable place—my bedroom perhaps?'

'Jacques, please!'

He laughed. 'Oh, you are so delightfully English! I was only teasing. Off with you to your work, you temptress! I have to be in Theatre in ten minutes and I must clear my head of all wicked thoughts and concentrate for the next few hours.'

He leaned against the door after Liz had gone,

breathing deeply as he tried to restore himself to working mode. He shouldn't have made it so obvious that he still wanted her, but he found Elisabeth irresistible. There was something about her that he'd never found in any other woman.

A pang of sadness ran through him. If things had been different, if he could have offered Elisabeth a real future, she was exactly the sort of woman he would have loved to commit himself to for ever and ever and…

He tried to end that useless train of thought as he strode over to his desk. All he could offer Elisabeth was fun and romance. That was as committed as he dared to be. He hoped, with all his heart, that was all she wanted, too.

Liz had noticed Jacques's solemn expression as she'd left him and was impressed at how quickly he could change from teasing lover to responsible surgeon. She took deep breaths as she went down the corridor, trying to gather her thoughts. It was only as she reached the entrance to A and E that she realised she hadn't given Jacques a firm decision about tonight. She would have to call Gina to see if it was possible.

'Good morning, Doctor,' a large, navy-blue-uniformed sister called. 'We were expecting you. The patient in cubicle two has been waiting longer than the others if you wouldn't mind examining him. I'm Sister Catherine. *A bientôt.*'

The blue uniform disappeared into the treatment room. Liz moved quickly into cubicle two. The young nurse who'd taken her to see Jacques was standing beside the examination couch, giving the patient a glass of water. She smiled when Liz walked in.

'Hello, Dr Liz. Have you come to examine my patient?'

'Yes, Béatrice. Have you got the case notes? Excellent.' She glanced at the top sheet. Claude Demarque, age 35. Someone had scrawled underneath the time of admission, 'Patient appears inebriated. Check blood for alcohol level.'

'Has anyone taken a blood sample, Béatrice?'

'Not yet, Doctor.'

Liz smiled down at her patient. 'Hello, Claude. How are you feeling now?'

'I'm fine when I'm lying down, Doctor. It's when I stand up that I go all dizzy. I was taking my daughter to the holiday playschool and I just sort of fell over as I was leaving her. It was so embarrassing. One minute I was walking towards the door and the next I was hit by a wave of dizziness. Suddenly I found myself on the floor. And then without warning I started to feel sick. One of the assistants held a bowl under my head just in time. When she called an ambulance they asked me if I'd been drinking.'

'And had you been drinking, Claude?' Liz asked quietly.

'Drinking? At nine in the morning? I had a glass of Bordeaux with my supper last night but that's all.'

Liz had a hunch he was speaking the truth but she thought she'd better make sure. Anyway, she needed a blood test to check out what else her patient might be suffering from. The symptoms he described could be indicative of a more serious condition.

'I'm just going to take a blood sample, Claude,' Liz said.

Béatrice handed her a sterile packet from the examination trolley before rolling up the man's sleeve.

Liz inserted the needle and drew off the required amount, before placing three specimens in different containers, carefully labelling them for the tests she would require.

'Would you take these along to the pathology lab, Béatrice, please? I'd like the results as soon as possible.'

She sat down in the chair beside the examination couch and started to take a more detailed case history.

'Tell me about yourself, Claude.'

'Not much to tell really.' The man put a hand behind his head and raised himself up on the pillows. 'I'm thirty-five, married, have a son of eight and a daughter of four. I'm a computer salesman but I'm on holiday at the moment.'

'Has anything like this happened to you before, Claude?'

The patient hesitated. 'Once or twice, well, quite a few times recently, but not as bad as this. I've managed to keep it from my wife so—'

'Why would you want to keep it from your wife?' Liz asked gently.

More hesitation. 'Marie worries about things like this. You see, her brother died of a brain tumour. Sometimes, when I go all dizzy, I can't see or hear properly. I start to sweat, then sometimes I vomit. I usually know when an attack is coming on and I get myself to the bathroom and lie on the floor until it passes. Sometimes it lasts only a few minutes but once it was a couple of hours. When I came out of the bathroom I told my wife I must have eaten something bad in the canteen at work.'

'Claude, I'd like to do a series of tests on you, but you mustn't jump to conclusions. You may be worrying unnecessarily. There are a number of conditions that might be sparking off your symptoms.'

'I'd like to go home as soon as possible and, Doctor, please, don't tell my wife I've been here.'

The man was swinging his legs over the side of the examination couch as he prepared to leave. Liz put a detaining hand on his arm.

'Claude, I'm afraid I must ask you to stay. We need to get a clearer picture of your illness…yes, hear me out. You are ill, and until we can make a firm diagnosis and treat you, these attacks will continue to plague you. Please, think about it. You can't go on pretending that all is well. Sooner or later…'

'OK.' Claude lay back against the pillows. 'I suppose you're right.'

'I'm going to admit you for further tests so we need to contact your wife.'

Claude stared up at Liz. 'Don't tell her I've got a brain tumour.'

'Claude, we haven't made a diagnosis yet. Let's be optimistic about this. You're simply here for a few tests.'

The patient smiled at Liz for the first time. 'Thanks, Doctor. I'll put myself in your hands.'

Liz smiled back. 'Now, just lie still. Béatrice is back from the path lab now and she'll look after you while I arrange your admission.'

The rest of the day was taken up with a variety of cases. That was what was so challenging about A and E. One minute you were quietly getting on with routine work and the next there were several emergency admissions that put everybody on their toes.

In the middle of the day there was an explosion in a nearby quarry and Liz and her colleagues found themselves dealing with four badly injured workmen who had to be admitted to the orthopaedic ward. She was relieved that all of them would survive, but the extent of their injuries meant that they would require expert medical care for several weeks to come.

By the end of the afternoon, the strain of working hard all day was beginning to tell. Liz took a couple of minutes off to phone Gina. She hadn't had a minute to herself all day. She was relieved to find the A and E office empty as she dialled her sister's number.

'Of course I'll babysit,' Gina said. 'Clive's planning to work on his book and Mum's going to the Theatre with Sidonie so it'll be just Melissa and me. I bought her a new video today when I was shopping in St Gabriel.'

'You're so good to her, Gina.'

Gina laughed. 'Don't be silly. I love looking after Melissa. You've both brightened things up since you came back home.'

'Well, thanks a lot. I won't be late.'

'Be as late as you like. Are you going out with anybody I might have heard of?'

'Possibly. Can't talk here.'

'Oh, Liz! I thought so.'

'Look, Gina, I've got to go. I'm still technically on duty. Bye.'

As she hung up, she felt a pang of sadness for her sister. Poor Gina! She would make an ideal mother. Her dream was to have a large family and it just hadn't happened. One of the reasons she'd given up working at the primary school had been because she thought she might conceive if she was at home with Clive and didn't have to rush out to work each day.

The door of the office opened. Jacques, still in theatre greens, pulled his cap from his head, allowing his unruly dark hair to flop over his forehead once more.

'Any chance of a cup of coffee for a poor, exhausted surgeon?'

Liz smiled. 'I think I could manage that if I could find some clean cups.'

Jacques reached into a cupboard above the cafetière of coffee that was retaining its heat on the hotplate below. 'There you go, Doctor.'

Jacques made for the nearest squashy armchair, tossing aside a couple of medical journals that were lurking amidst the cushions as he sank down into the depths of it.

Liz stepped across the long legs he'd stretched out in front of him and placed the two cups of coffee on to a small table.

'At last a quiet moment,' she said, as she took a sip of her coffee.

'Been like that for you, too?'

Liz nodded. 'I've just realised I haven't had any lunch.'

Jacques smiled. 'Neither have I. All the more reason why we should go out and have a superb dinner. I know just the place. You are going to come out with me to-night, aren't you?'

'Yes, I just phoned my sister and…and told her I wouldn't be home for supper.'

Jacques smiled. 'Sounds like you have to ask permis-sion to be out for the evening.'

She hesitated for a second. 'Well, Gina does most of the cooking so it would be discourteous not to tell her I won't be in.'

'So, have you had any interesting cases today, Elisabeth?'

'My first case is still a bit of a puzzle. A man came in after suffering vertigo, nausea and vomiting. He said it's happened before and sometimes he goes deaf and can't see properly for a while. I've admitted him to the medical ward and ordered the usual tests. I've got a hunch...'

She stopped. Jacques was listening intently to what she had to say.

'Go on, what's your hunch?'

'Well, it could be Ménière's disease.'

Jacques nodded. 'That's what I was thinking.'

'Were you? For a surgeon you're very perceptive.'

Jacques laughed. 'Ménière's disease is no longer simply a medical condition that patients have to put up with. When I was working as an ear, nose and throat surgeon I studied all the latest techniques for dealing with this condition. I spent a year in the States where I learned how to do an operation which, in many cases, can cure the condition.'

'I read about that in *The Lancet* but I've never met anyone who's actually performed the operation. You obviously know a great deal more than I do about Ménière's disease. I've treated patients in a more conservative way so...'

Liz broke off, realising that Béatrice had come into the office and was standing close by, listening to what she was saying.

'Do you want some help, Béatrice?'

'No, I was just trying to learn about Ménière's disease. I've heard of it but I don't know much about it. Something to do with a disturbance of the inner ear, isn't it?'

'Yes, that's right,' Jacques said. 'Pull up a chair, Béatrice, and let me tell you something about it.'

Jacques waited until the young nurse was comfortable before continuing.

'We don't know what causes the disease but it's believed to result from the pressure of increased levels of endolymph, the fluid in the inner ear. This leads to varying degrees of vertigo, tinnitus and deafness. No two cases are alike and it's very difficult to diagnose.'

'Can it be treated with medication?' Béatrice asked.

'We can control the attacks with a variety of drugs. These act to reduce abnormal signals coming from the balance organ in the ear and help to relieve nausea and vomiting.'

'What about surgery?'

'Surgery can be used to drain the endolymphatic sac, which is the small receptacle that removes waste products from the inner ear.'

'So that would reduce the pressure, wouldn't it?' Béatrice said.

Jacques nodded, pleased at the young nurse's interest. 'Yes, it would.'

'Is that the operation you would perform?' Liz asked.

'Not exactly. I've found the best treatment involves an injection of gentamicin, an antibiotic that is toxic to the inner ear, directly into the nerve endings of the middle ear. The treatment is controversial because in a few cases the hearing can be damaged. When I was in the States, doctors developed a catheter with a bulbous tip which could be placed inside the eardrum next to the inner ear. This means that the concentration of the drug can be controlled more easily. The success rate is now much higher.'

'When we get the results of our tests back, and if our patient is diagnosed as having Ménière's disease, would you be able to give that treatment, Jacques?'

Jacques leaned against the back of the chair. 'Of course. But let's get the diagnosis established first.'

Sister Catherine, who'd come in while Jacques had

been talking, poured herself a coffee and joined the group.

'It's not often we have a teaching session in my office, Jacques. Thank you very much.'

Jacques stood up, unhooking the theatre mask that was still entwined around his neck. 'And thank you for the coffee, Sister.'

He turned and looked down at Liz. 'See you later. *A tout à l'heure, Elisabeth.*'

Liz could feel the blood rushing to her face as she stood up and made her way across the room towards the door.

'Thank you for all your help today, Dr Elisabeth,' Catherine said.

Liz turned at the door, willing her complexion to remain a normal colour. 'I've enjoyed my work. I'm going off duty in a few minutes. Is there anything you'd like me to do before I go, Sister?'

'No, we're all quiet again. And, please, call me Catherine.'

There was one further patient Liz knew she wanted to see. All day she'd hoped to have time to go up to the children's ward to check on Michèle, the near drowning case. She'd promised the girl and she would be expecting her.

'Hi, Michèle, how are you today?'

The young girl gave a broad smile as Liz arrived at her bedside. 'I'm fine, Liz. A bit tired. That's why they're making me rest today, and also the blood tests were a bit funny.'

Liz sat down on the side of the bed, noticing the strained expression on her young patient's face.

'What do you mean, Michèle?'

Michèle raised her hand and waved at a passing nurse. 'What is it I've got?'

The nurse came closer. 'Michèle has diabetes mellitus. She didn't know about this before but…the notes are all here, Doctor.'

Liz scanned the notes quickly. Apparently the various tests were conclusive. She reached across the bed and squeezed Michèle's hand.

'It's a good thing we found this out. You'll have to stay in for a few days until we've got you stabilised and then you'll be able to go home and look after yourself.'

'I'm not worried about it, Liz. Mum explained that, because I'm ten, I can do my own testing at home and work out how much insulin I'll need. She'll help me at first and after that it will just become routine.'

Liz smiled. 'That's my girl!'

'You know, I've been feeling a bit weird lately. My head was all fuzzy when I was swimming yesterday and I think I sort of blacked out even before I sank down into the water. I'm a good swimmer. I would never have got into difficulty like that if I hadn't been ill.'

'Well, I'm glad Jacques was able to save you.'

'And you helped to pull me round as well, didn't you? Maman told me all about it. Thanks for everything you did.'

Liz stayed to chat for a little while longer before saying goodbye, promising to return the next day.

Jacques caught up with Liz as she was walking down the corridor that led from Paediatrics.

'Can you meet me in the car park in ten minutes?'

'Make it fifteen, Jacques. I need a shower.'

'So do I.'

Liz smiled. 'But you don't need make-up.'

'Neither do you, Elisabeth. I remember that morning at dawn, as the sun rose over the sea. You looked—'

'Jacques, please!'

'That's the second time you've reprimanded me today, Elisabeth. OK, I'll behave myself while I'm still here at the hospital.'

Jacques stopped her and whispered softly into her ear. 'So, that shower. Do you want to come with me?'

He flashed her a wicked grin and headed off. Liz found herself fighting back a smile. The man was incorrigible but so infinitely exciting! She took some deep breaths. The two young nurses who had been walking behind her now passed by and glanced across at her. One of them said something to the other and they started to giggle. Was it so obvious that she was in the middle of a most unsuitable liaison? That she was about to go out with the one man in the world she should be avoiding?

It was madness to go out with Jacques tonight! Totally unrealistic to imagine that she could possibly control her emotions. Even if she could control her own emotions, what about Jacques? He was showing all the signs and symptoms of a man hell-bent on eventual seduction. If not tonight then at a later date.

She sighed as she went into the staff cloakroom, found a shower cubicle and stripped off. She should be the happiest woman alive to be going out with the man of her dreams. Couldn't she just pretend, for one evening only, that this wasn't going to lead to trouble? Couldn't she simply live for the moment as she had done five years ago?

'I wish!' she said out loud as she turned on the shower.

CHAPTER THREE

'WHERE are we going, Jacques?'

'Do you really want to know? I'm planning to surprise you.'

Liz looked out of the window at the sheer drop from the cliffside road. 'In that case, don't tell me.'

'We're going to watch the sunset from one of my favourite restaurants over the other side of the hill.'

Liz watched the disturbingly sexy smile appearing on Jacques's face. He seemed to be having his own private thoughts as he steered the car up the narrow winding road.

'Penny for them?'

'What do you mean?'

'It's a silly English phrase which means I'd be willing to pay for your thoughts.'

The smile broadened. 'I was thinking how surprised my father would be if I were to turn up at our family restaurant tonight. He's a very perceptive man. He asked me the next day—the day after you came to our restaurant—if he was going to have the pleasure of meeting you again.'

'And what did you say?'

'I told him no, because you were married. So my father would be more than a little surprised if I took you back to our restaurant.'

'What makes you think he would remember me, Jacques? It's nearly five years ago.'

Jacques took one hand off the wheel and placed it over

hers. 'Oh, my father would remember you all right. He's still got an eye for a beautiful woman. With your shining, long blonde hair and your lovely face, my father wouldn't have forgotten you. I remember that when I told him you were married he said, '*Quel dommage!* What a pity!'

'But, Jacques, you were due to be married in a couple of weeks!'

'My father didn't like Francine. I think he was still hoping there was time to save me from…how do you say it? A fate worse than death. That's what he said ever since Francine moved in with me. When he came up to Paris to stay with us he told me she wasn't the woman for me.' Jacques paused. 'But he liked you.'

'Jacques, we mustn't talk like this. We're just friends who…' She closed her eyes, trying to make sense of the unfolding situation. 'Friends who've been lovers.'

As she leaned back she knew she wasn't handling the situation as she'd meant to. She'd walked straight back into Jacques's life and he had no idea that she still wasn't free to enter into a relationship with him. Not the kind of relationship he would want. A child-free relationship where enjoyment and pleasure, freedom to travel, to be simply a couple without any kind of parental responsibility, seemed to be of paramount importance to Jacques.

As if realising that she was having problems coming to terms with their new situation, Jacques began to speak in a quiet, soothing voice, reminding her of that evening when they'd first met.

'When you came into the restaurant, I remember looking up from the table where I was serving and realising that I wanted to get to know you. It was like *un coup de foudre*, as we say in France—I think you say a bolt of lightning or something like that when your heart seems to stop and you feel a great shock wave going through you and—'

'Jacques, I—'

'No, let me finish.' Jacques was gripping the wheel. 'When I brought you that cognac as you sat alone on the terrace, I hadn't intended to stay more than a few minutes chatting to you. I just wanted to be near you for a short while, but in the end...'

Liz watched him shrug his shoulders as the memories flooded back.

'In the end we spent the night together,' she said softly. 'Neither of us intended it to happen but...Jacques, it mustn't happen again.'

She saw the clouded expression on his face as he tried to concentrate on the road ahead. Suddenly he swerved over to the edge of the road and parked close to a gap in the hedge that surrounded a field.

He put his arm over the back of her seat and moved closer to her.

'What is all this about, Liz? Why can't we at least have something together? That night meant a lot to me. That was why I decided that I didn't truly love Francine. So why can't...? Unless there is someone else. Tell me, Elisabeth. Is there someone else?'

'No, but there are reasons why I prefer not to commit myself. I can't explain. I can't...'

'I don't want you to commit yourself, Elisabeth! I want you to stay just as you are. Free as the wind!'

Liz swallowed hard, almost overwhelmed by the nearness of Jacques's face to hers. His lips, his sensual mouth were so close to hers. Free as the wind! That was how he wanted her to be. That was the problem. If he only knew just how far he was from knowing the truth about her life.

'You must stay free and uncommitted, Elisabeth. I want nothing from you except the pleasure of your company. I'm free and uncommitted myself. That's why we get on so well together. We have no commitments other than our work as doctors. We work hard and play hard. And while we're playing together we can have fun, lots of fun! Oh, Elisabeth, all my life I've wanted to meet someone like you. And when I first found you I was forced to say goodbye too soon...but now...I can't believe you're back!'

'I'm not the woman you think I am, Jacques.'

'You're exactly as I remember you and that's all I ask for.'

He drew her closer, bringing his lips down on to hers. She sighed as she gave in to his gentle kiss. As his kiss deepened she closed her eyes, abandoning all her resolutions to act otherwise but trying to convince herself that this was just a simple kiss. It wasn't going to lead any further. Jacques had said he didn't want any kind of commitment, so she was quite safe to have a little uncommitted fun with him.

Perhaps even a light-hearted affair? As the thought passed through her mind she could feel her treacherous body reacting with excitement at the prospect. Well, what harm would it do to live dangerously for a while?

Jacques was pulling away, his eyes intent on her face, searching for any sign that she was displeased with the passionate way he'd kissed her. No, she seemed perfectly happy with the way things were going. He'd established that there was no one else, so maybc he was rushing things too much. Perhaps he should hold off a little—if he could!

He moved back, adjusting himself to a more comfortable position. Either he needed to buy a larger size of trousers or else he should stay away from this enticingly sexy woman. Simply being near Elisabeth had sent his libido rocketing sky high!

He was already in a high state of sexual tension. His whole body felt as if it wanted to explode unless he could make love to Elisabeth. But he had to control himself. He mustn't rush into a sexual liaison tonight. It was too soon. They must get to know more about each other first. Last time he'd been too precipitate and it was understandable that Elisabeth should want to take things more slowly. He mustn't blow it now that he was being given a second chance.

He took a few deep breaths to calm himself before starting the engine. As he drove down the other side of the hill to a tiny village, nestling at the foot of the cove, he could see the lights of the cottages twinkling near the bay. Concentrating on the steep gradient and the hairpin bends brought him back to his senses.

He'd reserved a table in the window of the small restaurant overlooking the bay. The head waiter showed them to their seats, handed them menus and asked about drinks.

'A bottle of sparkling mineral water and a bottle of champagne,' Jacques said.

He raised his glass towards Liz after the champagne had been uncorked. 'To our reunion…so unexpected!'

Liz smiled as she drank the heady champagne. 'Is that why we're drinking champagne?'

'We don't need an excuse to drink champagne. Every day is a celebration of life.' He lifted the bottle from the ice bucket and began to top up her glass.

'Careful! It's going to my head.'

Jacques put down the glass. 'We don't need to drink the whole bottle. I shall only have one glass. I have to drive back up that precipitous road, not to mention the fact that I'm on call at the hospital tonight. I simply wanted to mark this special occasion because I want to remember it...just as I remember vividly that night we spent together.'

'So do I.'

Liz sipped her drink as she looked out across the water. The sky was dark now, except for the light shining down from the moon, high above the cliffs. Somewhere near the horizon, she could see the lights of a ship.

'I remember walking into your father's restaurant feeling terribly alone because I didn't really want to be there. My sister Gina had booked a table for four people, but there was a crisis in my brother-in-law's family and they had to fly back to England that day.'

Liz leaned back in her chair, toying with her glass, momentarily thinking how her life would be different now if she hadn't gone out that evening and met Jacques.

'Then my mother's friend Sidonie phoned to say don't forget she'd booked theatre tickets for that evening. My mother is hopeless at remembering where she's supposed to be. I wanted to cancel the table, but Gina persuaded me to go to the restaurant alone. She said it wouldn't be a good idea to stay in, brooding about how I was going to cope with my two-timing husband.'

'You'd left your husband in England, I remember.'

'I'd come out to my mother's house so that I could decide what I wanted to do.'

The waiter was standing close by, waiting to take their order. Jacques said he was going to start with the giant prawns in a garlic butter sauce.

'It's a *spécialité de la maison*,' he explained.

'Sounds super. I'll have that, too.'

'And then...' Jacques was still studying the menu.

'The lamb is particularly excellent here. Yes, I'm going to have the *gigot d'agneau.*'

Liz smiled. '*Gigot d'agneau* is a favourite of mine. I like the meat nice and pink, if there's a choice.'

Jacques finished explaining to the waiter and turned back to give Liz his full attention again. She intended to say no to the second glass of champagne but somehow it appeared anyway. She was feeling deliciously mellow already, rather like the champagne.

'I remember you walked into the restaurant and my father went to meet you.'

'The tall, grey-haired man. He had a lovely welcoming smile. Nice teeth for a man of his age.'

Jacques laughed. 'Careful what you say. I may get jealous. My father brought you across to a table near the window. As he passed me he told me to take great care of you because you were a woman alone and that was unusual for someone so beautiful.'

'Ah, so the care you lavished upon me was simply at your father's instructions, was it?' she teased.

He smiled and shook his head. 'I found it impossible to stay away from your table. When you went out onto the terrace for your coffee I made a point of taking a long time with my final duties so that many of our guests had left. Only when you were almost alone out there and looked as if you might escape at any moment did I dare to offer you a glass of cognac. I was surprised when you accepted my offer.'

Liz laughed. 'So was I! I opened my mouth to decline and then I sort of thought, Oh, what the hell!'

Jacques repeated 'What the hell!' very softly in English.

With his attractive French accent it sounded delightful. Liz took another sip from her glass. Just like the last time they'd been in a restaurant together, she wanted the evening to go on for ever.

'I remember we poured out our hearts to each other as we sat on your terrace overlooking the sea,' Liz said softly.

The waiter was clearing their starter plates. She waited until he'd gone before she spoke again.

'It seemed strange that we were both in disastrous liaisons, wondering whether we should end our relationships.'

Jacques leaned across the table and placed his hand over hers. 'We both had so much in common. I think it was fate that drew us together that evening.'

'Oh, Jacques, don't say…' She stopped as the waiter returned to serve the next course.

Jacques withdrew his hand but his eyes across the table held such loving tenderness that Liz could feel herself already melting with suppressed emotion. How would this evening end? Like the last one? If her body was anything to go by now, she would find Jacques impossible to resist.

She looked down at the succulent lamb on her plate, toying with a tiny piece, willing her appetite to return. She was starving but talk of that other evening was turning her thoughts to a more exhilarating appetite for love.…

'Is the lamb to your taste, Elisabeth?' Jacques asked. 'Not too pink? In England when you ask for pink meat it is cooked slightly longer than here in France.'

'Jacques, I'm half-French, remember?'

Jacques laughed. 'I know, I know. But I think you have lived longer in England than in France, *n'est-ce pas*? Tell me about your French mother.'

'Karine is in her early sixties, looks about ten years

younger and enjoys life to the full, in spite of having had one minor heart attack and being on medication.'

'Perhaps that's why your mother enjoys life to the full, because she knows how precious it is.'

'That's one reason, I'm sure. But before my father died he made us all promise that we wouldn't mourn him after he was gone. He told us to enjoy every minute of our lives because you never knew how long you'd got.'

'He sounds like a wonderful father.'

'He was. If only he'd admitted he was ill he might still be here. He didn't tell anyone he thought he might have a problem until a couple of months before he died of cancer of the colon.'

Again Jacques put his hand over hers, squeezing her fingers in a comforting gesture.

'It's so sad when an illness could perhaps be cured and it's left too late.'

'I was particularly devastated because, as a doctor, if he'd only spoken to me about his symptoms I…' Liz removed her hand, lifted the starched white napkin and brushed the corners of her eyes.

'Enough of that! Dad told us all to carry on with our lives as if he were still with us. That was seven years ago. A year later my mother had a cardiac arrest. Fortunately Sidonie was with her. She got the ambulance very quickly and a paramedic saved my mother's life. We all came out to France and suggested Karine sell the house and come back to live in England so that we could take care of her.'

'But your mother preferred to remain in France?'

Liz nodded. 'She begged us all to come and live with her in France. Dad bought the house about ten years ago when he finally retired from being a university professor and this was where my mother wanted to stay. My sister

Gina and her husband love France as much as I do so they came to live here with my mother. I held off coming out permanently for a long time, for various reasons, but this year they all persuaded me to join them.'

The waiter was holding out a menu of desserts which Liz declined. She'd enjoyed the delicious lamb, but now she simply wanted to go on talking to Jacques. Just as she had done that first time. Well, there was no harm in just talking.

Jacques told the waiter they would take their coffee out on the terrace that overlooked the tiny harbour.

As he took Liz's hand and led her from the table, Jacques asked if she would like a glass of cognac to go with her coffee.

She smiled. 'No, thanks. It's all becoming too much like a replay of five years ago, isn't it?'

Jacques held out one of the wicker chairs beside a small table on the terrace and waited until she was comfortably seated amid the cushions.

'No, it's not a replay of five years ago,' he said softly, holding her attention with the dark, enigmatic expression in his eyes.

'This is for real, Elisabeth. This is you and I, enjoying the present. But there's nothing wrong in remembering the past. Especially when we thought it was simply a once-in-a-lifetime experience. Do you remember how we walked out on to the beach holding hands as if we'd known each other all our lives?'

Liz sighed. 'How could I forget?'

Their table was near the edge of the terrace, open to the fragrant night air. It was all too reminiscent of that other terrace where she'd lost her heart and forgotten she had to live in the real world. Just as she was in danger of doing now.

Out there across the tiny harbour she could see the moonlight glinting on the water, lights twinkling in a couple of boats moored until the morning. The smell of the sea wafted up to her, that indefinable fresh, exciting scent that brought back so many happy memories, not just of that other evening but of the many happy times she'd spent close to the sea during her childhood, adolescence and when she'd been pregnant with Melissa.

She'd been apprehensive about the future during those last few weeks of her pregnancy, she remembered, and Gina and her mother had persuaded her to come out to France to stay in the family house. She'd had baby Melissa in a large hospital further along the coast because the hospital at St Gabriel hadn't been built four years ago.

She'd taken maternity leave from the London hospital where she'd been working. When it had been time to return to London she'd felt so sad to be leaving this lovely part of the world. Walking in a London park wasn't as uplifting as walking by the sea when you had a problem to think through.

She took a sip of her coffee. 'One thing I still can't understand about the night we first met was how I could have done something completely out of character like walking out on the beach at two in the morning with a relative stranger,' she said softly almost to herself, as if it was a continuation of her thoughts.

Jacques pulled his chair closer.

'I must admit, that worried me at first. I mean, I could tell you weren't the kind of girl who simply took off with a stranger, without worrying about what might happen to her. I simply wanted to be with you a little longer when I suggested we walk on the beach. I wanted to show you the beautiful night sky, the endless tapestry of stars, the fabulous moon illuminating everything and…' He broke off, the catch in his voice giving away the fact that some of the emotion from that other occasion was still haunting him.

'I'd never seen such a beautiful sky, Jacques. I remember walking hand in hand, barefoot—you were carrying my shoes as well as your own, weren't you? We walked into the sea, turning back when the water had reached my knees. It was sheer madness, but such an escape from the pressures of the previous weeks when I'd known I had to come to a decision about whether to forgive Mike or not.'

'It was a terrific release for me, too. I hadn't given Francine a single thought during the whole evening. And when we sat down on that rock at the far end of the beach…'

'It was still warm, wasn't it, Jacques? Even though it was the middle of the night the rock still retained its heat from the sun's rays. And then when you kissed me…well, it seemed so natural that we should…'

Liz hesitated, unable to explore the poignant memory any further. It had been the most wonderful experience of her life and she should never try to put it into mere words.

'I remember feeling as if we were the only people on the planet as dawn broke,' Jacques said quietly. 'We were Adam and Eve at the beginning of time.…'

Jacques looked up as the waiter placed two large glasses of cognac on the table, indicating that they were on the house.

Jacques picked up his glass and raised it towards Liz. 'It would be impolite not to taste the cognac. But I must only have a small sip so that—'

His mobile phone rang. Liz watched his expression

change to one of professional competence. He'd told her he was on call. Perhaps this was the call that would save her from having to make a very difficult decision tonight.

Jacques cut the connection. 'I'm wanted back at the hospital. Some kind of problem with Claude Demarque.'

Liz was immediately alert. 'The patient I admitted this morning? We discussed the possibility that he might have Ménière's disease, didn't we? What's the problem?'

Jacques was already on his feet, signalling to the waiter that he wanted the bill.

'Night Sister says Claude wants to sign himself out. His wife is there with him and she's hysterical because she's sure he must have a brain tumour. Claude wants to convince her he's OK by going home. It's a complicated situation and Night Sister wants me to help sort it out.'

Liz stood up. 'Do you want me to come with you?'

Jacques hesitated. 'You're not on call, Elisabeth. You don't have to—'

'I know that, but would it help if I was with you? I may be able to take care of Claude's wife while you're dealing with Claude.'

Jacques nodded. 'Yes, I'd like you to be there. You were the one who admitted Claude. You saw what he was like when he first came in.'

The bill was paid and they were back in the car, climbing the hill to return to St Gabriel. Liz leaned back against the soft leather of the seat as the car purred up the hill. It was a powerful car that coped with the gradient as if they were running along a flat motorway.

'I think we should tell Claude we believe he's got Ménière's disease,' Liz said quietly. 'Before I came away tonight, I went to the medical ward and checked on the results of the tests so far. It's a difficult disease to diagnose, but if Claude was told he could simply be suffering from a disorder of the inner ear, it may put his mind at rest.'

Jacques stared ahead at the darkened road. A car was coming towards them. He kept close to the side, dipping his lights.

'It would certainly be more reassuring than worrying about the possibility of a tumour,' he said. 'We could tell Claude about the treatment for the condition—if we could be sure our diagnosis is correct. I think it would be a good idea for Claude to have a CT scan as soon as possible.'

'I've already ordered one,' Liz said. 'Claude was in a bit of a state when I left him this afternoon, so I put in an emergency request for a scan this evening.'

'Brilliant!' Jacques squeezed her hand. He was slowing down as they reached the outskirts of St Gabriel. 'We can check it out ourselves when we get there. I only hope we're correct in our diagnosis. If not…'

'At least we'll know the worst. A brain tumour isn't the end of the world. It can sometimes be treated if it's caught in time.'

'Of course it can. It's a pity that Claude's brother-in-law wasn't treated earlier. These bad experiences always cause distress to the families.'

Liz looked up at the approaching façade of the Clinique de la Côte. It looked different at night. With its shiny white stone and endless illumination, it looked like the flagship for a chain of five-star hotels instead of a place where life-and-death decisions were made.

Liz had time to grab her stethoscope and a white coat from her locker before she hurried along the corridor to join Jacques in the medical ward.

Night Sister hurried down the ward to meet them as

they waited beside the desk near the door. The patients' lights had all been extinguished and the light from the desk cast a soft glow. After the hustle and bustle of the day, the ward seemed unnaturally calm and quiet.

'We've put Claude in a private room,' the navy-blue-clad figure explained in hushed tones. 'His wife is with him. I've persuaded her to stay calm until you come but she might start shouting again, in which case…'

Jacques put his hand on Sister's arm. 'Don't worry, Danielle. We'll do all we can to keep the peace. I know you don't want your patients to be kept awake. Now, have you had the results of the CT scan that Dr Elisabeth asked for?'

'CT scan? That must have been before I came on duty and the day sister didn't mention it. She said there were ongoing tests. Just bear with me a minute…'

The middle-aged sister rummaged through a pile of case notes, X-rays and other papers on the desk, adjusting her spectacles and moving the direction of the desk light so that she could see more clearly. She'd been planning to go through all this information when she had a quiet minute but she'd been rushed off her feet ever since she'd arrived on duty.

'Ah, here it is. Yes, Claude Demarque…'

'Thanks, Sister.' Jacques took out the printed slip that accompanied the scan. A few succinct sentences demolished the idea that there could possibly be a brain tumour.

Jacques smiled. 'Claude's brain is absolutely normal! Let's go and tell Claude the good news.'

Claude looked up expectantly from his bed as the two doctors went into his room. His wife leapt to her feet, knocking over the chair she'd been sitting on.

'It's bad news, isn't it? You've found something. Go

on, you can tell me. I was brave when they told me about my brother and—'

'Madame Demarque,' Jacques began calmly, but the overwrought woman came towards him, grabbing his arms, sobbing loudly.

'Tell me, tell me, Doctor....'

Liz put an arm around the woman's shoulders and gently detached her from Jacques. 'Come and sit with me here, *madame*.'

She pulled two chairs close together. Mme Demarque seemed to calm at the sound of Elisabeth's soothing voice.

'We have good news for you,' Liz said, in a calm, confident tone. 'The scan has revealed conclusively that Claude doesn't have a brain tumour.'

'Oh, oh...'

Liz allowed herself to be hugged, before once more trying to calm Marie. Claude was looking relieved but, characteristically, he was keeping his emotions under control.

'I've told Marie why I was brought in here,' Claude said quietly. 'From the tests I've had today, have you any idea what's causing my symptoms?'

Jacques sat down on the side of the bed. 'You have a perfectly treatable condition called Ménière's disease.'

Jacques proceeded to explain all that this involved just as he had done earlier to Nurse Béatrice.

'And this operation you spoke of to correct the tension in the inner ear, will you be able to do it, Dr Chenon?'

'I most certainly will.'

Marie had calmed down and was now taking an interest in what was to happen next.

'*Et vous*, Dr Elisabeth? Will you be helping Dr Chenon to sort out my husband's problems?'

'I'll do all I can when I'm not required to work somewhere else,' Liz said, carefully.

Jacques looked across the bed at Liz. 'If I scheduled you to assist me in Theatre, would you be willing?'

She swallowed hard. 'Of course.'

So long as she simply concentrated on the task in hand she could forget that she and Jacques had ever been close—for the duration of the operation at least.

'Bon!' Jacques smiled as he stood up, coming round the bed to put a hand under Liz's arm so that he could guide her towards the door.

'I'll ask Sister Danielle to come and see you,' he told Claude and Marie. 'Would you like to stay the night, Marie? There's another bed in this room. I'm sure it can be arranged.'

'Thank you. I'd like that. I'm too overwrought to go home.'

'I'm going to prescribe a light sedative for you, Marie,' Liz said. 'You've had a difficult time and it will help you to sleep.'

Marie stretched out her hands towards Liz. 'Thank you both so much. You've no idea how relieved I feel. Yes, I think I will feel much better when I've had a good night's sleep. And now that I know that Claude is in good hands...'

She turned to smile at her husband as she went to sit on the edge of his bed.

Jacques held open the door for Liz and they went back into the ward to speak to Sister Danielle.

Once Jacques and Liz were outside in the car park, they kept the interior light of the car on for a while as they discussed their patient.

'We're not out of the woods yet, but I'll take charge

of the case and see it through,' Jacques said. 'I'll have a conference with the medical firm tomorrow and find out the best way of working together on this case.'

He switched off the light and started the car. 'Now that's settled, how about a little *pousse café* back at my father's restaurant? We didn't finish our cognac before we left the other restaurant and—'

'Jacques, I don't think so.' Liz shook her head.

Jacques was holding the car steady at the exit from the hospital, waiting until it was decided which way he should drive.

'Why not?'

'Because...' Liz searched around for a plausible excuse. How could she say that she daren't reignite the flames of their passion for each other? And she knew that's what would happen if she let down her guard.

'Look, if you don't want to stay out late, I'll take you home,' Jacques said in a decisive tone. 'Which way?'

Liz gave directions and Jacques moved the car forward.

She glanced across at the uncharacteristically stern profile. 'It's getting late, Jacques, and—'

'Please, Elisabeth, you mustn't feel you have to apologise for wanting the evening to end here. It's your choice. You're a free agent. I'm happy to have spent a few hours with you.'

She leaned back in the seat, feeling like a child who'd got hold of a pin and pricked the balloon. Everything had been going so well between them and she'd chosen to kill their wonderful rapport stone dead.

But that was what she'd planned to do, wasn't it? To make it quite clear that they couldn't revive their mad relationship. How could she distance herself from the fact that she was the mother of Jacques's child if she allowed herself to get carried away again? If she went back for a drink with Jacques, everything would start again. They would most surely walk along the beach, holding hands, and then…

A shiver of sensual excitement ran down her spine.

'Are you cold, Elisabeth? I'll adjust the air-conditioning,' Jacques said, pressing one of the switches on the mahogany dashboard.

They were reaching the house, driving in through the wrought-iron gates, tyres scrunching on the gravel drive. It would be polite to invite Jacques in for a nightcap, but how could she? Supposing Melissa was sitting downstairs drinking hot chocolate with Karine and Gina as she often did if she awoke late in the evening. How would she explain that?

Oh, by the way, Jacques, this is your daughter. I know you don't like children but don't worry about it, everything's under control.

Under control, my foot! Liz sat rigidly still as Jacques moved around the front of the car to open the passenger door. He was polite but distant as he stretched out his hand towards her.

'Goodnight, Elisabeth.'

'Goodnight, Jacques.'

She lifted her face towards his. Their cheeks touched in the French way of saying goodbye. But they may as well have been brief acquaintances. Even so, Liz felt the strangulated passion deep inside her stirring with an unwelcome demand for consummation. She knew she could reverse her hard-line decision if she…

But Jacques was already pulling away from her, his face set in a solemn expression that showed he was capable of making a decision and sticking to it, even if she wasn't.

It was time to move on. Liz didn't turn around as she hurried from the car towards the front door. Jacques was already back in the car, driving away along the curve of the drive, scattering gravel towards the flower-beds in his haste to escape the embarrassing situation.

Driving down the road, Jacques headed for the sea, not stopping until he found a quiet, deserted part of the road that ran along the edge of the beach. As he cut the engine he leaned back, clenching and unclenching his hands.

What had he done wrong this evening? It had all been going so well. Even when they'd been working together in the hospital he'd felt himself enveloped in the warm, sensitive rapport that had built up between them during the precious hours they'd been together. He'd been sure he would by now have been taking Elisabeth in his arms and she would have been responding to his caresses as she had done before.

What was holding her back? She'd said there was no one else but maybe she hadn't been telling the truth. Or perhaps he'd come on too strong tonight. Yes, that was probably the problem. She wanted to go more slowly. Well, he could be patient. They could simply be friends. No more talk about that first wonderful evening together. That was just too heart-rending and too disturbing to contemplate. What they'd had that night had been something too special to repeat.

But deep down he was sure that Liz was withholding something from him. She was decidedly cagey when she talked about her family. Always on the defensive, chattering too quickly as if there was something to hide. Yes, Liz definitely had a secret she didn't want him to know about.

From now on he would pretend they'd only just met, that they hadn't spent a night together that had seemed like a whole lifetime in terms of loving experience. He would pretend that he didn't feel as if he'd known her all his life.

Gina opened the door as she heard the car driving away.

'Liz! Was that…?' She lowered her voice. 'Was that Jacques?'

Liz nodded. 'Oh, Gina, it was so awful not being able to invite him in for a drink or something. I felt so mean, so deceptive, and I completely spoiled the whole evening by being horribly standoffish at the end.'

Gina closed the door behind her sister. 'Come in the kitchen and tell me all about it.'

'Is Melissa asleep?'

'Of course. Mum and Clive went upstairs ages ago. It's past midnight. I just wanted to wait up and hear how it went. Drink?'

'I'd love some hot chocolate if that's not too much trouble, Gina.'

'No trouble at all. I'll have some myself.'

Gina was fishing in the fridge for the milk, smiling happily now that her younger sister was safely home.

Liz sank down on to a chair. 'You're so good to Melissa and me. I don't know what we'd do without you.'

'Nonsense!' Gina poured milk into a saucepan and lit the gas. 'It gives me something to do. I feel as if I've got a proper job again now that I look after Melissa while you're working.'

'Gina, I've been wanting to ask if you'll let me pay you something for the time that you take care of—'

'Don't be silly! You're my sister, for heaven's sake, and looking after Melissa is sheer bliss. I wish she was mine—oh, I know I shouldn't have said that. It sounds as if I'm trying to take your place but I'm just the most doting aunt in the world. When my own babies come along…'

Gina broke off. She was mixing the chocolate in a jug and she stopped stirring as she stared out through the kitchen window into the darkness. 'Liz, I will have babies one day, won't I?'

Liz stood up and went over to put an arm around her sister's shoulders. 'I hope so. You'd be the best mother in the world. Have you thought anything more about having some tests at the hospital? See if there's any reason why you aren't conceiving?'

'I've thought a lot about it but Clive doesn't want us to go down that road. He says if nature intends us to have children they'll arrive sooner or later. If not, he's happy to just be a couple.'

'But you're not, are you?'

Gina turned round and hugged her sister. 'No, I'm not, but I love Clive so I'll go along with whatever he says. It would be silly to try to talk him into something he doesn't want to do.'

Liz pulled away and grabbed the saucepan as the milk rose to the top. 'Oops! Nearly didn't make it.'

She poured the milk on to the chocolate, took the spoon from Gina and began stirring. 'Well, if Clive does change his mind…'

'Liz, stop worrying about me!' Gina was dabbing a tissue over her eyes. 'I've got my darling niece to look after and my little sister back home with me, so what more can I ask for? You've got enough problems of your own to sort out. Talking of which, how did the evening go—before you decided to bring it to an abrupt end?'

Liz placed a mug of chocolate in front of her sister and sat down at the kitchen table, cradling her own mug.

'It was fabulous! Absolutely fabulous. We fell back into the same kind of rapport we had five years ago. It was as if I hadn't been away.'

'Except you're now the mother of Jacques's child,' Gina said.

'Gina, you have no idea how I wanted to tell Jacques about Melissa! It seemed so right to be with him. I couldn't bear to think of him being Melissa's father and not knowing about it. It's so unnatural. I feel so guilty at not telling him the truth and—'

'Hey, steady on, Liz!' Gina put her mug down on the table. 'Don't get carried away into any sentimental ideas about playing happy families. Jacques told you he doesn't want children. He's chosen to be childless. We've been through this so many times and it always comes back to the same problem. Some men want babies, some don't, and you're unlucky to have found a man who doesn't.'

Liz cradled her head in her hands with her elbows on the table as she stared down at the well-scrubbed wooden surface. There was the deep cut where her father had dropped the meat knife in the middle of carving a huge joint of beef because the cat had just brought in a dead mouse and her mother had started screaming.

'I know, I know! I kept on reminding myself all through the evening when we were getting on so well. One word from me about Melissa and that would be the end of our relationship.'

Gina nodded. 'I'm afraid you're right. Just stick with that idea and you won't go far wrong. Enjoy going out with Jacques but, for heaven's sake, don't tell him about Melissa.'

Liz lifted her head up and stared at her sister. 'But, Gina, I simply don't know how long I can go on living a lie! Deep down inside me I'm convinced I've got to tell Jacques!'

CHAPTER FOUR

GINA leaned forward and squeezed her sister's hand in a comforting gesture. 'Liz, you're tired and overwrought. In the morning—'

'In the morning the problem will still be there,' Liz said as she tried desperately to take stock of the situation. 'It's difficult at the hospital. I'm making new friends. Sooner or later the question of family will crop up and I'm so proud of my lovely daughter, I'll want to tell everybody about her.'

'I know, Liz,' Gina said gently. 'I'm only trying to think of ways to make things easier for you. As I see it, you're in an impossible situation and—'

'Gina, it's almost as if I'm ashamed of Melissa...but actually I want everyone to know I've got a beautiful daughter. And yet I've deliberately not mentioned her in front of my colleagues, though they're bound to find out about her sooner or later.'

Liz gave an anguished sigh. 'I've always been an honest kind of person. It goes against my nature to keep quiet about Melissa. And, anyway, on my days off I'm going to take Melissa out and about with me. I desperately want to spend more time with her. I'm missing so much of her growing up while I'm working.'

Gina was looking thoughtful. 'I really would like to help you solve the problem. Wouldn't it be possible to say you have a daughter but imply that she's Mike's child? That's what Mum and probably everybody else assume anyway. You didn't divorce Mike until months after you'd been out here in France and met Jacques, did you?'

'Gina, I'm trying to be honest with myself and—'

'Well, I'm only trying to think of how revealing the truth would affect everybody concerned, Liz. It seems to me that Jacques, a self-confessed non-family-type man, wouldn't take kindly to shouldering his responsibilities. The situation between you and Jacques would become intolerable and you'd miss out on any chance of a real friendship with him. As for Mum…well, she'd be horrified if she thought you'd been lying to her.'

'Gina, we've been through all this before,' Liz said patiently.

She knew her sister meant well by offering all this advice. She loved Gina dearly and she'd always looked up to her as the elder sister, but sometimes she needed to remind Gina that she was grown up and wanted to make her own decisions.

'Mum would survive the revelation if she had to, Gina,' Liz said.

'But would she?' Gina said in a concerned voice. 'I'm not so sure. I know you're the doctor, but I spend more time with Mum than you do and I've seen her struggling to walk up the stairs sometimes.'

'You didn't tell me this!'

'Well, I didn't want to worry you. Anyway, Mum's due for another cardiac check-up next week so we'll find out how she really is then. Meanwhile…'

Gina leaned across the table and squeezed Liz's hand. 'Meanwhile, looking at it from all angles, my advice to you, my darling little sister, is to keep quiet. Don't rock the boat.'

Liz felt as if she was in limbo for the next couple of weeks. She'd told Gina she wouldn't reveal anything until she was absolutely sure what the right course of action was for everybody concerned. But every time she tried to come to a decision she found herself unsure, worried about the effect a revelation would have on her mother, unwilling to risk losing Jacques's friendship and making things worse than they already were.

As far as seeing Jacques was concerned, that problem seemed to have resolved itself. She certainly hadn't gone out of her way to speak to him and Jacques himself seemed to be more elusive than before. In fact, she suspected he was avoiding her.

Going about her work at the hospital, she occasionally came into contact with Jacques. They were polite with each other, nothing more. For Liz it was as if her heart was bleeding inside. That evening, which had started so well and ended so badly, had been nothing more than a situation where two friends had tried to resuscitate the past. But because she'd been so unsure of how she was going to handle the situation she'd checked any possibility of an advance in their relationship.

Walking into the medical ward to check on Claude Demarque, she couldn't help remembering that evening when she and Jacques had told their patient he didn't have a brain tumour. Their patient's wife's infectious happiness at the revelation had blended with the general mood of optimism that they'd all enjoyed. But only a short time later she'd deliberately changed all that.

Liz pulled up sharply as she saw that Jacques was standing beside the bed, chatting to his patient. He appeared to be saying goodbye. Yes, he was now leaving. She would be able to speak to their patient if she held off for a while.

She hovered beside one of the empty beds in the ward.

Claude had been moved into the general ward while he was undergoing more tests to confirm the diagnosis and prepare him for eventual surgical intervention. It was a busy medical ward where doctors came and went, and it looked as if Jacques hadn't seen her as he made his way to the door.

'Elisabeth!' Jacques paused, his eyes registering surprise. He moved towards her.

'I've got a few minutes' break from A and E,' Liz said quickly. 'I wanted to see how our patient is…sorry, how your patient is getting on, Jacques.'

She raised her eyes to his and saw the flicker of dismay that flashed across his face.

'I've been meaning to have a talk with you about Claude,' he said. 'I hope you don't feel that you've been sidelined and kept in the dark about this case.'

'Not at all,' Liz said, feeling quite the reverse. 'I love working in A and E and I'm sure you've got this case under control. I just wanted to see how things were progressing. I admitted Claude to the hospital, so I'm taking a special interest in his care, even though I'm obviously no longer on the case.'

Liz glanced across at Claude, a short distance away. He'd put his headphones back on and was listening to the radio, his head resting on the pillow, his eyes closed, unaware that he was the subject of discussion.

'Liz, I'm sorry if I've offended you,' Jacques said quietly, putting his hand under her elbow and drawing her towards one of the windows at the side of the ward. 'I've been in a difficult position, having to liaise with the medical firm. The question of having you assist at the actual operation—'

'Jacques, it's OK!'

She tried to smile, but her lips felt too tight. What happened was more like someone baring their teeth.

'I've been getting all the information from Claude and from reading the case notes whenever I've popped in,' she told him. 'You're going to do the operation and it really doesn't matter who assists you, does it?'

'Oh, but it does!'

Liz held herself in check as she wallowed in the wonderful, melodious sound of his authoritative voice. Ask me to assist you, a wicked little voice inside her was prompting. Go on, ask me, please! I just want to stand near you in Theatre and feel all that power radiating towards me from every pore in your tantalising body...

'Are you OK?' Jacques leaned towards her.

'I'm fine!' She ran a hand through her hair. This time she actually managed to smile.

'We've scheduled the operation for next week. Are you still willing to assist me in Theatre?'

Liz swallowed hard. Jacques had enquired if she was still willing. Meaning, no doubt, that now that they were barely on speaking terms, would she be able to work with him?

'I'd like that very much. I think I could learn a lot.'

She turned away as she thought how naïve she sounded! Like a junior medical student trying to ingratiate herself with the senior professor of surgery so that he would give her a good mark in the practical exam!

Well, no harm in continuing what she'd started.

'Thanks very much, Jacques,' she said in a cool, polite tone. 'I'll go and see Claude now.'

'Just a moment, Elisabeth. I was wondering if we could get together on Sunday when we're both off duty?'

She could feel her heart fluttering at the prospect but

she knew she had to remain cool. 'I'm not sure. I'll have to check my diary.'

It was breaking her heart to be so obtuse, but she was playing for time until she could sort out how she was going to cope with the situation.

Her mother's appointment with the cardiac specialist had been reassuring. The consultant had pronounced that Karine was as healthy as could be expected. But Gina had still advised Liz not to make any drastic revelations in the near future.

Jacques cleared his throat. 'OK, give me a call on my mobile if you're free on Sunday. If not, some other time. Oh, by the way…'

Liz had been walking away, going down the ward again. She stopped to listen to what he had to say.

'I met your sister yesterday. I knew immediately it was your sister because you're so alike. She was in St Gabriel, shopping, and she was talking in English to her little girl so I knew she must be your sister.'

Liz held her breath for a couple of seconds. 'Did…did you speak to my sister?'

'Of course I did! She was looking in a shop window and, from behind, I thought it was you. I'd called your name and by the time your sister turned round I had to say something to explain my mistake. I introduced myself and she told me her daughter's name was Melissa. What a lovely child! She had a packet of sweets and she took one out, unwrapped it and gave it to me.'

'Gina didn't tell me she'd seen you.'

'She must have forgotten.'

'Actually…' Liz paused. It was now or never. She couldn't go on lying about Melissa.

The ward seemed to have gone completely quiet. She was only aware of Jacques standing in front of her, a perplexed look in his eyes. For the rest of her life she would remember this moment.

She swallowed hard as she started again. 'Actually, Melissa is my daughter, Jacques.'

Jacques's eyes widened in amazement. 'You didn't tell me you had a daughter.'

'I didn't think you'd be interested.'

'Oh, come on, Liz! You told me about your mother and your sister but—'

'I didn't think you'd be interested because you said you didn't like children.'

Jacques frowned. 'When did I say that?'

'Oh, the first time we were together. You said that you and Francine had decided that children didn't fit in with your lifestyle. And when we met up again this time you obviously hadn't changed. You said you didn't want a family.'

'Yes, but that's different to not liking children. I like other people's children. It's just that—'

Jacques's bleeper went off. 'I've got to go. Let me know about Sunday as soon as you can, so that I can make other plans if you're not available.'

Liz watched him hurrying away down the ward. The cat was well and truly out of the bag now but she'd only told half the story.

Half the story was all Jacques could have—for the foreseeable future. Jacques didn't object to other people's children, apparently. Well, that was a step in the right direction. Maybe if Jacques got to know Melissa, found out how wonderful she was—well, he'd already said she was a lovely little girl—maybe they could build on that. And when she was brave enough to tell him that Melissa was his, he would…

She couldn't stretch her imagination any further. What she would want would be a miracle to happen.

Fat chance! She gave a big sigh, knowing full well that she was living in cloud cuckoo land. People's characters didn't change—especially men! Jacques was an independent individual who loved his freedom, and the revelation that he had responsibilities he hadn't known about wouldn't be a good idea.

But, sooner or later, she was convinced that she would have to make the revelation and take the consequences. So she may as well enjoy this brief period when they were still good friends.

She clutched her stethoscope as she made her way across to Claude's bed. Her patient smiled as she approached. He pulled himself up on his pillows and removed his headphones.

'Hello, Elisabeth. I hoped you were coming to see me. I saw you talking to Jacques and I thought you might be discussing my operation.'

'We were, Claude. It's scheduled for next week, as I expect you've been told.'

Claude nodded. 'Can't wait to get it over with. I stumbled in the bathroom this morning and a couple of nurses had to help me back to bed.'

'So the medication isn't fully effective, then?'

'It helps. I'm better than I was, but I've got ringing noises in my ears now.'

Liz nodded, sympathetically. 'Ah, tinnitus. Yes, that sometimes happens in cases like yours. Well, hang in there. The operation should make a vast improvement.'

'I hope so, Doctor. Will you be assisting Jacques?'

'Yes. That's what I've been told.'

Claude smiled. 'I'll be in good hands with the pair of you working on me.'

Liz smiled back. 'We'll do our best, Claude.'

For the rest of the day, Liz was kept busy in A and E. There was a constant stream of patients coming in with minor injuries. Being the height of the tourist season, the little town of St Gabriel was inundated with tourists and if there was a medical problem they headed for the hospital rather than the local doctor's surgery.

She treated a man and his wife who were suffering from a mild case of food poisoning. After taking a case history, she decided that the culprit was probably a dodgy curry that the couple had eaten in a restaurant down the coast the previous evening. She gave them medication to get the vomiting and diarrhoea under control and after a short period of rest and rehydration treatment she allowed them to go home.

Shortly after that, Liz took care of a young man who'd skidded off his motorbike and fractured his tibia and fibula, the bones in the lower leg. Checking the X-rays confirmed that the leg would require surgery to set the bones in the correct position. This entailed liaising with the orthopaedic team and the operating theatre and admitting the young man to the orthopaedic ward.

Towards the end of the afternoon, she was confronted with a suspected cardiac arrest. A young but rather large lady with chest pains was wheeled in, clutching her chest. It turned out to be a false alarm but Liz assured the distraught patient that she had been quite right to come to the hospital and make sure.

She was able to assure her patient that her heart was in excellent condition but it wasn't a good idea to go climbing on the cliff path with her young family immediately after a large lunch.

If she was to lose weight, that would also help, Liz added, as she always did in cases like this. So many people nowadays were endangering their health by eating themselves into an early grave.

The overweight lady pulled a wry face and explained that she'd been trying to lose weight ever since the birth of her first baby. But now, three children later, she was bigger than she'd ever been. But she was still trying.

'Well, that's the main thing,' Liz said carefully. 'Keep trying. We do have a clinic here where you will be given advice and—'

'I've got a diet sheet, Doctor,' the woman said, hauling herself off the examination couch and walking slowly out of the cubicle. 'I'm going to go home and stick to it. I really am.'

'Such determination! You've obviously made a great impact on your patient.'

Liz leaned back, her hand clutching the edge of the examination couch as Jacques walked in.

'Oh, I have a great impact on everybody who comes into contact with me,' Liz said facetiously.

'So I've noticed.'

Jacques was looking down at her with an enigmatic smile on his face. She could feel her body reacting to the closeness of him. They were quite alone in here. She realised with a pang of lust that she wanted him to lean forward, take her in his arms and do something most unprofessional that was probably a sacking offence in France as well as in England.

'I'm still waiting for your call, Elisabeth.'

'Sorry?'

'You were going to look in your diary and let me know if…'

'Oh, yes, Sunday.' She hesitated. 'No, I can't. It's the

only day this week that I can spend with my daughter and—'

'Bring Melissa with you! We'll do something she'll enjoy. How about we have lunch at the family barbecue my father organises at his restaurant?'

'I'm not sure if—'

'My father arranges a lunchtime barbecue every Sunday and all the families who come simply love it. We have a Bouncy Castle in the garden, and on the beach there are a couple of helpers who organise games for the children, rather like the Club Mickey. Did you ever go to the Club Mickey when you were a child, Liz?'

'Yes, yes, I did.'

She could feel herself being won over. She knew Melissa would absolutely adore being part of a great crowd of children, but what about herself? Wouldn't it all be too impossibly difficult to cope with? All that guilty angst nagging at her until she couldn't stand it any longer and simply blurted out the truth!

'Liz, I can't think why you're taking so long to decide,' Jacques said testily. 'What is there to think about?'

'What indeed!' If only he knew!

'Was that a yes?'

Oh, what the hell! Liz nodded. 'A definite yes, and thank you very much for asking us. Melissa will be thrilled, I'm sure.'

Jacques gave a relieved smile. 'And if the rest of your family would like to join us for lunch, I'm sure—'

'No. No, thank you,' Liz said quickly. 'I've no idea what they're all planning to do. Clive will probably be writing or he may have a literary meeting. My mother often has lunch with friends, and Gina…well, my sister has lots of interests.'

'Well, if we don't have time to talk again, I'll see you

on Sunday,' Jacques said. 'Do you remember the way to my father's restaurant?'

Liz smiled. 'Oh, yes.'

The road to the restaurant was etched in her memory. She'd never been able to forget even the tiniest detail of that fateful evening, however hard she'd tried over the past five years.

'Would you like me to collect you?'

'No, thanks. I've bought myself a little car, so I'm completely independent.'

Jacques took a step forward and placed his hands on either side of her arms, drawing her closer to him. She held herself still, willing her heart to stop thumping so madly. She ought to move away but she was riveted to the spot by some imaginary chains around her legs. She didn't want to move but she wanted to eliminate the gap between herself and Jacques and simply melt into his arms, moulding herself against his hard, infinitely exciting, utterly desirable body....

'Completely independent,' Jacques repeated, in a cool, sexy voice. 'Yes, you're a girl who likes her independence, Liz, aren't you? Can't think how that ex-husband of yours ever persuaded you to marry him, let alone have a child together.'

Liz stiffened. Her throat felt dry. Her head was spinning. 'Mike and I were very young when we married. I was totally naïve, and as for having a child...'

'Jacques!' Sister Catherine bustled into the cubicle. 'Thank goodness you're still here. Will you have a look at this patient who's just been brought in with abdominal pains? I would very much value your opinion because I think we should...'

Liz breathed a sigh of relief as Jacques and Catherine disappeared.

What had she planned to say to Jacques? What could she say? She hated all forms of deceit and by prolonging the lie she couldn't get rid of her awful feeling of guilt. The tension was building up like a dam about to burst. She had to act soon before she became overwhelmed by the impossible situation her secrecy was imposing.

'So where is this place we're going, Mummy?'

Melissa gave Liz a beguiling little smile as she un-twirled the ribbons that Liz had just coiled up in preparation for the hairdressing session.

Liz reached for the ribbons and began coiling them up again. 'It's down by the beach, Melissa. Now, if you could just sit still for a moment…'

Melissa clapped her chubby little dimpled hands. 'The beach. Lovely! Can we take Mimi?'

'I don't think Mimi would like the sand. Cats prefer their own homes.'

'Well, I'll take Teddy, then.'

The little girl wriggled off her small chair and went over to her bed to extricate the battered teddy-bear from the depths of her duvet.

'Teddy wants his fur combed because he's coming with me. It's OK, Mummy. I can do it. Where's my comb? There it is. Keep still, Teddy! How many times have I told you to keep still when I comb you?'

Liz waited patiently until Melissa was back on her chair, clutching Teddy in one hand and a comb in the other. The bear-combing would keep her daughter relatively still. Liz never tried to hurry Melissa.

Their time together was very precious and she didn't want to spoil it by becoming a nagging parent, even though today, of all days, with her apprehension growing more intense by the minute, she could have done with a little more co-operation. But four-year-olds lived in a world of their own where such immaterial things like time didn't exist. Liz was feeling, at this moment, that she herself wished she was a four-year-old.

'Melissa, would you like plaits or a ponytail today?'

Liz continued brushing the long dark hair to make it shiny and manageable. It was the exact shade of the hair of the unnerving man they were going to meet for lunch. Would he notice? Mike, who took after his Spanish grandmother, had been dark-haired and brown-eyed, so no one seemed to have considered Melissa's colouring to be unusual.

But would Jacques look in the mirror, add two and two together and come up with the right answer?

'I'd like two bunches please, Mummy, like that big girl we saw on the telly. One up here like this…' Melissa grabbed a handful of hair and pulled it to the top of her head. 'And the other up here like—'

'Yes, I get the picture,' Liz said, patiently starting once more to tame the thick dark hair.

'Have you time to talk before you go, Liz?' Gina asked, leaning against the open door of Melissa's bedroom.

'Not now, Gina,' Liz said.

She and Gina had discussed her plans for Sunday lunch at great length the previous evening and Liz was in no mood to reopen the debate, especially in front of Melissa.

Gina smiled. 'I only came to say I hope you have a nice time.'

'We're going to the beach,' Melissa said excitedly. 'To a restaurant. It's got a garden with a Bouncy Castle and lots of children.'

Gina leaned forward and stroked Melissa's silky hair.

'It's going to be such fun. You must tell me all about it when you get back, Melissa.'

'Yes, yes. Hurry up, Mummy, and finish my hair and then we can go.'

'Be careful, Liz. Don't get carried away and say things you'll regret,' Gina said under her breath as she moved away.

'I'll just have to play it by ear,' Liz said quietly as she tied up one of the ribbons on Melissa's head.

Having Gina prompt her at every stage of this difficult situation wasn't helping at all. She loved her sister to bits but she wished she'd simply stay out of it.

When they'd been growing up together, Gina had always been a tower of strength. The elder sister with all the answers. The girl who'd been there, done that, had the T-shirt. Liz had looked up to her, admired her, always accepted her advice. Because Gina had always been sincere. She'd only ever wanted what she thought was best for Liz.

But Liz knew that she had to make up her own mind. Had to limit the damage already done by withholding her impossible secret from the one person who, although he wouldn't like it and would probably deny and try to avoid it, nevertheless should be told the truth.

'Elisabeth, this is my father, Pierre. Papa, this is Elisabeth and her daughter Melissa.'

'Enchanté!' Pierre Chenon bowed his head as he brought Liz's hand to his lips in a slightly outmoded but very gallant gesture.

Liz thought what a charmer the elder Chenon was! Tall and straight, he had a very striking, distinguished appearance with his thick grey hair slicked back behind his ears and the marvellous dark brown eyes twinkling with animated enthusiasm for life. Just like his son!

Pierre bent down. 'What a lovely little girl! Hello, Melissa. How old are you, my dear?'

'I'm four and a quarter.'

Ouch! Liz maintained the bright, polite smile on her face. Watching Jacques now, she could imagine him doing mental calculations as he smiled at Melissa.

'You're a big girl for your age,' Jacques said, squatting down on his heels so that his face was level with Melissa's. 'When I saw you out shopping the other day, I thought you were at least five.'

Melissa gave Jacques a beaming smile, reaching up with her chubby hand to touch his dark, already bristly face. She rubbed her hand over his cheek, seemingly enjoying the rasping feel.

'Did you really think I was five? That's nice. Did you like that sweet I gave you?'

'It was lovely,' Jacques said solemnly.

'I've still got some in the bag at home. I was going to bring them with me but Mummy didn't think it was a good idea because we're going to have lunch, aren't we, and you shouldn't take food into a posh restaurant, should you? What are we having? I'm very hungry.'

'What do you like for lunch?' Jacques asked.

'I like everything,' Melissa said, patting her stomach. 'Everything except oysters,' she added quickly.

'I tried one once when Grandmaman was having a party with her old friends and it sort of got stuck in my throat and my mummy had to tip me upside down and pat me on the back. The oyster came out but I was sick all over Mummy's new suit.'

Jacques was holding back laughter. 'Was Mummy cross?'

Melissa looked puzzled. 'No, she was pleased I'd got rid of the naughty oyster.'

'So, no oysters, then,' Jacques said solemnly.

'No oysters,' Melissa repeated. 'Do you like my new sandals? I chose them myself. Red's my favourite colour.'

'We're going to have a barbecue,' Pierre said, smiling down at the chatty little girl.

He was very impressed with the way Melissa could switch from French to English without apparently noticing it, just like her mother. She was as beautiful as her mother as well, but her colouring was a complete contrast.

He hadn't known that the lovely Elisabeth was married when she'd walked into his restaurant that last time. When Jacques had told him that Elisabeth was married he'd felt it was such a pity. The two of them had seemed to get on so well in the short time they'd been together, even though Jacques had been working for part of the time.

Pierre reached down and held out his hand towards the little girl. 'Would you like to come with me and watch me start the barbecue? I'm going to select the steaks and fish that will be grilled above the charcoal. You can choose the portion you would like.'

'Ooh, yes, please! Have you got chicken?' Melissa asked. 'I like chicken. What's the piece I like best, Mummy?'

'The breast.'

'Yes, that's it. Yummy!'

'Let's go and choose a nice portion for you, Melissa,' Pierre said, leading the excited child away.

Liz looked up at Jacques, wondering if he was going to comment on Melissa's age.

Jacques was stroking his chin thoughtfully. 'Melissa is four and a quarter,' he said quietly. 'So you went back to your husband for one last fling, did you?'

The shrill sound of Jacques's mobile couldn't be ignored. Jacques frowned as he listened to whoever was calling.

Liz held her breath as she waited. It was the hospital. An emergency of some kind. One of the junior doctors asking if Jacques would go in and give him some advice.

Jacques cut the connection. He looked down at Liz as he explained that he would be back as soon as he could, suggesting that she carry on and start lunch without him.

Liz tried to hide her feeling of guilt and apprehension as she looked up at Jacques. His expression was enigmatic, giving nothing away. He would be back soon. For once, she didn't want him to hurry. She wanted to compose her thoughts and do the decent thing. If she told him today, she would put herself out of her misery.

As she watched Jacques hurrying away, she knew that she would end one set of problems only to open up another, even more difficult situation. But whatever she had to do, she didn't want to hurt anybody, least of all Jacques and Melissa.

Melissa had always accepted that her father didn't live with them. Liz had never lied to her daughter. When Melissa had begun talking and asking if she had a daddy, Liz had said yes but he couldn't be with them. Melissa had been perfectly happy with the explanation when she'd been very small because she was always surrounded by family. But as she grew older she would start asking more searching questions and Liz knew that, sooner or later, she would have to tell her the truth.

So she'd better enjoy the brief state of limbo she was in! Because it couldn't last much longer.

She found Melissa standing by the barbecue, helping Pierre to put the portions of meat on the grill. Pierre had provided a stool on which Melissa could stand. The little girl even had her own child-sized apron with the logo of the restaurant emblazoned on the front.

'I have ten grandchildren,' Pierre explained as he turned over a large piece of steak with an iron spatula, 'so I have to have aprons for when they visit. Four children from my two daughters who live near St Gabriel. Six children from my two sons who live in Paris. None from Jacques, of course.'

'Why do you say ''of course''?'

'Jacques and Francine weren't interested in having a family. Jacques always said it would spoil their lifestyle. But I don't think that was the only reason. There's more to it than that— Oops! Careful, little lady!'

Pierre grabbed hold of Melissa's hand as she stretched out to touch one of the pieces of chicken.

'That piece is very hot. You'll burn your fingers.'

Pierre put down his spatula and beckoned to a man in a large white hat who was busily coating some steak with a specially created sauce.

'My chef will take over here, Elisabeth, while I play host to two charming young ladies. What a pity my son had to go to the hospital! But his loss is my gain. This way, my dears…'

As she followed the elder Chenon, Liz found herself wondering what other reason there could possibly be for Jacques to avoid having a family. The main point that had registered with her was that even Jacques's own father had accepted the fact that Jacques wasn't a family man.

Unlike his father, who seemed to revel in being at the centre of a large family. Liz was enthralled by the stories

ensure that nothing went wrong in the post-operative phase.

Jacques glanced at his watch. He'd been away from Liz for over an hour. He hoped his father was being a good host. Having finally persuaded Liz to spend Sunday with him, it was bad luck that he'd been called away. Still, she was a doctor and knew that these things happened if you took your work seriously.

As he started the engine of the car, Jacques was thinking how unfortunate it was that he'd been called away at that precise, important moment. Just when he'd been trying to digest the fact that it had been four and a quarter years since Melissa's birth.

When he'd begun to talk about this with Elisabeth, her eyes had held that haunted, worried look she often had. As if she was hiding something.

He put his foot on the accelerator and moved the car slowly forward. That would have made the period of conception around the time that he and Liz had made love, not once, not twice, but—

He gasped out loud as the memories came flooding back. He must stop tormenting himself! If he hadn't known it was impossible for him to father a child, he would have been tempted to believe that Melissa was his. That lovely long black hair, those dark eyes—so like the picture of his mother. Probably like his own if he looked in the mirror.

He felt a surge of anguish that what he was fantasising about was utterly impossible. He'd only imagined that Melissa's eyes looked like his mother's. He'd given way to a moment of utter make-believe. What if…? Wouldn't it be wonderful if…?

There was the sound of an ambulance siren. He pulled into the side of the road to allow it to overtake him on the hill. Another emergency somewhere. There were enough staff in A and E to cope.

He switched his thoughts back to Liz, resting his hands on the steering-wheel but not attempting to drive off. He was too overwrought to be safe on the road at the moment.

That night, that precious night, after they'd poured out their hearts to each other for such a long time, sitting on that warm rock, they'd swum in the sea, totally naked. It had all seemed so natural at the time. As if they'd known each other all their lives. And then he'd taken her hand and led Elisabeth out of the sea. She'd been dripping water, shaking herself like a mermaid drying her scales, all silvery in the moonlight. And she'd been laughing, laughing, running up the beach, teasing him to catch her.

As he had. He'd taken her in his arms, lowered her gently onto the sand and they'd made love again and again until…

Mon dieu! He really must stop bringing back these poignant memories. He must come back to the real world and stay there.

He took some deep breaths to steady himself. On a purely practical level he remembered that, at the risk of ruining the erotic ambience, he'd managed to slip on a condom each time they'd made love. But that method of protection wasn't one hundred per cent reliable, so maybe…

So maybe a child could have been conceived in those circumstances. But not by him. Not by a man who'd been told categorically by two different specialists that it was impossible for him to father a child. That serious bout of mumps when he'd been a medical student had definitely put paid to his chances…unless…

It was a big unless. A most unlikely unless. For two

years, during his relationship with Françine, they hadn't used any form of contraception. Francine had insisted she couldn't stand condoms. Francine had pointed out, most vociferously, that Jacques's sperm count was zero and as they were living together in a stable relationship, they didn't need to worry about using protection.

So, after a two-year relationship with no contraception, didn't that prove that he was sterile? But was it worth checking out?

He turned on the engine.

Perhaps.

CHAPTER FIVE

'YOU'RE back! What was the problem at the hospital, Jacques?'

Pierre stood up as he welcomed his son.

Liz pushed her coffee-cup to one side and smiled up at the two men. She was still worried about how she was going to answer Jacques's question about whether she'd gone back to Mike for one last fling, but she'd had time to formulate a reply. And it seemed that she ought to answer his question truthfully. So she was bracing herself for the right moment. And the inevitable recriminations that would follow.

'Oh, it was nothing that my junior doctor couldn't have handled if he'd had a little more confidence. But I prefer the junior staff to err on the side of caution.'

Jacques looked down at Liz. 'I hope my father has been taking care of you.'

'Pierre has been a most attentive host.'

The older man put his hand on his son's shoulder. 'I must go back to the kitchen for a while and find out how things are going. Are you ready for your lunch now, Jacques?'

'Do you think one of the staff would make a chicken sandwich for me and bring it out here? It's too late for a full-blown lunch.'

'Of course. And what about you, Elisabeth?' Pierre enquired solicitously. 'Would you like some dessert now?'

'No, thank you, Pierre. I'm fine.'

Jacques sank down into a wicker chair beside her. They were at the exact same table where they'd sat on that first evening but he wasn't going to think about that.

Liz looked out towards the garden. 'Melissa's having a great time. She comes back now and then to tell me she loves the Bouncy Castle or she's going to play in the sandpit. This was such a good idea.'

Her voice trailed away. 'Why are you looking at me like that, Jacques?'

'Like what, Elisabeth?' he asked gently.

'I think you know what I mean.' She swallowed hard. 'If there's something you want to ask me, please, go ahead.'

Jacques took a deep breath, but at the last moment he changed his mind. This wasn't the place for a showdown.

Yes, the timing of the conception seemed to indicate that Melissa might have been conceived that night if he hadn't been diagnosed as sterile. It was all pure, nebulous speculation. He couldn't ignore the fact that he'd lived with Francine for two years without any form of contraception and he hadn't fathered a child. Didn't that prove the specialists had been right in their diagnosis?

Supposing Elisabeth had gone back to her husband for one last fling. Had he any right to ask her such a personal question? There was also the possibility that she might have found someone else soon after they'd spent the night together. Understandably, Elisabeth must have been in a very vulnerable mood during that period when she'd been breaking up with her husband.

He reached across and took hold of her hand. She seemed to flinch at the touch of his fingers. She was expecting him to quiz her. There was no doubt that she had something to hide, something she didn't want to reveal.

He had to regain her confidence, make her trust him again. He loved her so much he couldn't bear to see her looking so worried. But this had decided him as to what he must do next.

He would go and see a fertility consultant and check out if there was the remotest chance that his sterile condition had reversed itself over the years. It did sometimes happen. Miracles did occur. But he wasn't going to raise his hopes too high. Not until he'd checked it out with the experts.

At the moment, with the medical condition he assumed he had, it would be an impossibility to offer Elisabeth a real future. Sooner or later, Elisabeth would want a man who could give her siblings for Melissa and, as far as he knew, he couldn't do that. But if by some wonderful quirk of nature, his medical condition had been reversed then a future would be possible, if Elisabeth loved him as much as he loved her.

And the possibility that Melissa might be his very own child… He drew in his breath, hardly daring to allow himself to dream too much about such an amazing possibility. Until he'd checked it out he had to remain calm, as if nothing had changed.

He smiled. 'There's nothing I want to ask you, Elisabeth,' he said quietly. 'Except would you and Melissa like to come for a walk with me on the beach when I've eaten my sandwich? We could walk along to the jetty where I've moored the boat and then have a short sail on the water if Melissa's not too tired.'

Liz could feel relief oozing from her every pore. 'We'd love to have a walk on the beach. I'll just go and collect Melissa.'

* * *

'Am I really steering the boat?' Melissa asked, her eyes wide with excitement as she held onto the rudder.

'You most certainly are,' Jacques said, his large hand enveloping the little girl's as he kept the boat on a steady course.

Liz leaned against the back of the wooden seat, revelling in the feel of the wind ruffling her hair. Over on the horizon she could see another boat, a much larger boat, speeding along in the bright afternoon sunlight. It looked like a cruise ship of some kind. She preferred their own little boat, simply chugging along at a slow pace, as if time had stopped still for all of them.

Looking at father and daughter now, laughing together as they steered the boat, she felt a lump in her throat. This was how life should be for them. Just the three of them in their happy family unit. But Jacques didn't want a family. He'd told her so himself and everybody who knew him acknowledged the fact. Even his father, especially his father. But Pierre also suspected there was some other reason for Jacques not wanting to have children.

What other reason?

She sighed as she lazily drifted her hand over the side of the boat to dip it in the cooling water. At least Jacques had said he liked other people's children so perhaps that was why he and Melissa were getting on so well. Jacques was now steering the boat towards a small cove, Melissa still 'helping'. Liz marvelled at his patience. He would make a perfect father.

She turned away and looked out to sea again. Don't think about it. Don't torture yourself. Jacques's father had said he believed in fate. For the moment she was happy to go along with that philosophy. She didn't want to change the status quo. She would live for today and let tomorrow take care of itself.

Pierre had insisted they take a picnic basket with them, pointing out that Jacques hadn't had a proper lunch and Melissa had a good appetite.

'Melissa will be hungry again in a couple of hours,' Pierre had said as he'd handed them a large basket full of goodies from the kitchen.

As the three of them sat on the sand in a deserted cove at the end of a long hot day, Liz was glad that they'd taken Pierre at his word. Melissa was wolfing down a chicken sandwich as if she hadn't eaten all day.

Jacques was watching the little girl, an amused smile on his face. 'It's great to see her enjoy her food so much.'

Liz smiled. 'She was never a fussy eater.'

She shielded her eyes from the slanting rays of the sun. Looking at Jacques and Melissa now, it was such a dead give-away. Their looks, their mannerisms. She was glad there wasn't a mirror on the beach at this precise moment—it would point to the obvious truth about Jacques and his daughter.

'Like two peas in a pod,' she muttered under her breath as she began to collect up the picnic plates and glasses.

'Would you like one last swim before we go back, Elisabeth?'

Liz smiled. 'Why not?' She glanced at her daughter. 'How about you, darling? Do you want to come in the water again with your armbands on?'

Melissa had curled herself into a ball and closed her eyes. Her breathing was becoming more rhythmical, relaxing as only small children knew how.

'I'm sleepy, Mummy.'

Liz tucked a towel around the little girl, checking that her armbands were still securely in place.

'We'll have to stay in the shallows, Jacques, where we can watch Melissa.'

Jacques nodded. 'She won't come to any harm. We'll be near at hand if she cries out.'

As they went into the sea, Jacques took hold of Liz's hand. The touch of his fingers was unnerving. A pulse of excitement ran through Liz's body. They hadn't swum together since that wonderful night. The night that Melissa had been conceived. She turned to look at Jacques. A pang of tender concern, tinged with intense guilt, surged through her.

'Jacques…there's something…' Her voice faltered.

It had been such a wonderful day. Why spoil it now? Why make the revelation before she needed to? Keep up the pretence. Enjoy the tenderness that existed between the three of them as long as possible. When she chose to reveal the truth, it would be shattered completely, possibly never to be restored again.

Jacques was looking down at her, his expression one of intense tenderness. 'Liz, what is it?'

She took a deep breath. 'I just wanted to say how much I've enjoyed our day.'

He put his arms around her, drawing her close. She was wearing a bikini that Pierre's father had given to her when he'd heard they were going out in the boat. It had belonged to one of his daughters apparently but he'd said she wouldn't mind because it was too small for her since her last child. The bikini was too big for Liz and hung loosely around her slender hips, threatening to slip down at any moment.

Jacques was wearing a pair of black swimming trunks that barely covered his hips. He held her against him. Skin against skin. Mmm…she could feel Jacques's arousal against her body, matching her own. She felt as if she was turning into liquid fire.

She glanced towards the shore at their sleeping daughter before raising her lips to Jacques's. When he kissed her she moulded her body against the hard contours of his. She wanted him to take her, here in the water. To rip off her bikini, carry her into the sea and make love to her among the waves as if they were two primaeval creatures who lived in a marine kingdom at the bottom of the ocean.

But from the depths of her rambling, erotic thoughts she managed to dredge up a shred of normality. It wouldn't be a good idea to make love here, not with their daughter only a short distance away.

Panting with the effort of controlling herself, she pulled away, holding Jacques at arm's length. 'Jacques, I…'

Jacques was trying to regain his breath, finding it difficult to restore himself into an everyday state of mind. He was forcing himself to come back to earth, but how much longer could he hold off? Being close to Elisabeth and not being able to make love to her was agony, pure agony!

He adjusted his bulging swimming trunks. 'We'd better have that swim.' He gave her a rakish smile. 'The water should help to cool me down.'

They swam together a few metres from the shore, continually glancing back at the sleeping child.

Jacques swam close to Elisabeth, holding out one hand towards her. She took it, treading water.

'Elisabeth, it's so hard for me to be near you and not to be able to make love to you,' he said.

'It's hard for me, too,' she said, turning onto her back, as she gazed up at the blue sky. At least she could be utterly truthful about some things with Jacques. She couldn't disguise her own feelings any more.

He was leaning towards her in the water, one hand touching her face. 'Are you free tonight? After you've put Melissa to bed, I mean?'

She could feel the passionate excitement surging through her from the brief renewed contact with him. Simply a hand on her face was enough to ignite her smouldering passion.

'Yes, I've got nothing planned,' she whispered, suspending all her better judgement. 'I could get away later....'

He reached forward and brought his lips close to hers. Then gently, very gently he kissed her with such infinite tenderness that she felt her whole body beginning to melt with delicious anticipation.

'Until tonight,' he whispered as they started to swim back to shore together.

Liz had been in a heightened sense of awareness throughout the whole of the time she'd been getting Melissa ready for bed. Her feet were still some way off the ground and she hadn't succeeded in joining the real world. The thought that she was going to meet Jacques later that evening was colouring all her thoughts.

As she pushed Melissa's plastic boat backwards and forwards in the bath foam she was trying to justify the fact that she was prolonging this deliciously sensual rapport between herself and Jacques. One justification was that if Jacques came to love her as much as she loved him then perhaps he would react favourably to the fact that he was the father of her child, even though all his adult life he'd tried to avoid being a parent and the responsibilities that went with it. It seemed unlikely but not totally out of the question.

'You look like you enjoyed yourself today,'

Gina came into the bathroom, carrying a couple of glasses of wine. She often did this at the end of the day when Liz was bathing Melissa. The two sisters would sit on the edge of the bath, trying to avoid the splashes that Melissa sent up towards them, gossiping about how they'd both spent their day.

'Yes, we both had a great time, didn't we, Melissa?' Liz said, avoiding eye contact with her sister. 'Did you have a good day, Gina?'

'I managed to drag Clive away from his desk this evening and we went for a drive along the coast. We've only just got in and he's back in his study again. Never stops working on that book if he can help it. So, where did you go?'

'Jacques took us out in his boat, Gina,' Melissa said excitedly. 'It's like this toy one only a lot bigger. And Jacques let me steer it to a beach, but I fell asleep and only woke up when we got back to the car park at the restaurant.'

'Sounds like fun,' Gina said, watching Liz.

'Yes, it was,' Liz said, remembering the stolen kisses in the boat on the way back as Melissa had slept on. Her whole body was still in a state of arousal. She didn't want to run away from the frissons of love that were still pulsating through her. She wanted to anticipate the night ahead. Because when she chose to make her revelation everything would change. But for tonight…

'Did you have a long meaningful discussion today, Liz?' Gina asked anxiously.

Liz glanced at Melissa but she could see that her

daughter was completely oblivious to the boring adult talk as she played with her toys in the foamy bath water.

'I didn't rock the boat, if that's what you mean,' Liz replied quietly.

Gina gave her sister a relieved smile. 'Good girl. Keeping everything under wraps. Let's drink to that.'

She held out Liz's glass towards her.

Liz hesitated. 'I mustn't drink tonight, Gina. I've got to drive. Mum told me she was happy to babysit before you came in just now.'

Gina's eyes flickered. 'And does Mum know where you're going?'

'She knows I'm going out to see a friend, that's all.'

'Well, I hope you know what you're doing.'

'Gina, I'm a big girl now!'

Melissa looked up from the bath at the sound of her mother's raised voice.

'You're a very big girl, Mummy. Will I grow as big as you if I eat all my food up?'

The tense moment was shattered. Both sisters looked at each other and began to laugh. Liz held out her hand towards Gina.

'Please, don't worry about me, Gina. There's absolutely no need because—'

'I can't help it. You're still my little sister,' Gina said, clutching Liz's hand. 'I don't want you to get hurt.'

'I know what I'm doing,' Liz said.

Gina pulled a wry face. 'If you say so.'

Gina put down her glass on the edge of the sink and rolled up her sleeves. 'Go on, Liz, let me finish bathing Melissa and then I'll put her to bed. You get ready to go out....'

'Are you going out, Mummy?' Melissa looked up.

'Yes, do you mind?'

'Of course I don't mind! I've got Aunty Gina and Grandmaman and Uncle Clive to look after me. And they always spoil me and let me stay up late! And they give me chocolate biscuits with my cocoa, don't you, Gina?'

Gina gave her sister a sheepish grin. 'I'm afraid we do.'

Liz smiled. 'Ah, I see!'

'Can I stay up until you get back, Mummy?'

'No, I may be quite late. I may even stay the night.'

'Oh, is it a sleepover?' Melissa asked.

Liz hesitated, aware of Gina's anxious expression.

'It might be. I don't like driving home alone late at night.'

Melissa nodded as she pulled a solemn face like she'd seen her mother do.

'Quite right, Mummy. I don't think you should drive in the dark. There might be robbers or lions and tigers on the road. It's better if you stay the night and come back in the morning when it's daylight. Will you call at my favourite *boulangerie* and bring me a *pain au chocolat* for breakfast?'

Liz smiled. 'Of course I will, darling.' She dropped a kiss on top of her daughter's soapy hair before turning to look at her sister.

'And what would you like me to bring for you, Gina?'

'I'd just like you to bring yourself back all in one piece,' Gina whispered as she reached for the shampoo bottle. 'Come on, Melissa, it's time to have your hair washed.'

Liz looked up at the tall stone façade of the house. There was an impressive crenellated wall running around the edge of the roof and skirting a small tower that must command the most amazing views out to sea. It was much more imposing than she'd expected. Jacques had simply said he had a house further down the coast from St Gabriel. But this was a positive chateau!

Getting out of the car, she breathed in the fresh air. Mmm, she could smell the sea. She particularly liked a house that was near the shore. The seagulls were quiet now but she could hear the waves at the end of the garden if she stood quite still.

The front door was opening. 'Hello, Liz. You found the house!' Jacques sounded relieved. 'Any problems with my directions?'

'No, I just kept following the coast until I came to the village and then I turned off the main road, as you told me.'

She went towards Jacques, who was looking casual and relaxed in old jeans and a white polo shirt. He drew her against him and kissed her briefly on the lips.

She closed her eyes. The magic was still there, the magic they'd conjured up together in that little cove as their daughter had slept. It was funny how, more and more, she was acknowledging to herself that they were a family unit. But she was the only one of the three members of this family who knew the unit existed.

'Come inside.' Jacques put an arm lightly around her waist and led her towards the impressive oak door with its huge brass doorknocker shaped like a lion.

'It's a very grand house you're living in.'

Jacques smiled. 'It belonged to my grandmother. This was home to me when I was a child. I was the youngest and we didn't have a mother to take care of us, so when Dad bought the restaurant I used to get in the way. My brothers and sisters were able to help in the restaurant but I was too small.'

Jacques had taken her along a long corridor to the side

of the house. They were now in the kitchen. Liz looked around her at the high ceiling, the ancient wooden cupboards, the decidedly antique stove that ran along the wall at the back of this intriguing room.

'Come and sit down.'

Jacques drew her towards the table, before uncorking a bottle of wine.

'I shouldn't drink. I'm driving.'

This afternoon it had seemed inevitable that they would spend the night together but Liz wanted to make sure Jacques hadn't changed his mind. They'd both had time to cool down.

'I was hoping you'd stay the night. I do have a guest room,' Jacques added quickly, worried that he might be moving too fast.

He'd had no doubt about Elisabeth's strong feelings for him this afternoon, but she might be having second thoughts now.

Liz hesitated. Having brazenly told her sister she was coming home in the morning, she ought to carry it through. And the wonderful rapport that had existed between them was returning.

'I think perhaps it would be wiser for me not to drive home alone along the coast road,' she said.

Jacques felt relief flooding through him as he gave Elisabeth a seductively sexy smile. 'There's nothing wise about staying the night. It's what we both want, isn't it?'

His hands closed around hers. She felt the warmth of his skin torching her already heightened senses again. One spark from Jacques, that was all it took to ignite her dormant passion.

'It's what we both wanted this afternoon and nothing has changed as far as I'm concerned,' she said softly, revelling in the touch of his caressing fingers.

She looked up at the high ceiling. Unusual for a kitchen, it had an antique glass chandelier hanging from a central brass chain.

'Was that beautiful chandelier in place when this was your grandmother's house?'

Jacques smiled as he got up from the table to reach for a box of matches. 'It certainly was. I'll light the candles and it will become even more beautiful.'

He began to climb on the wooden table.

'Careful, Jacques!'

'Don't worry, I've been doing this from the time I could walk. One of my aunts or uncles would hold me up to the candle holders and let me strike the match.... There!'

'Oh, it's spectacular!' Liz clapped her hands together as she looked up at the now glowing chandelier.

Jacques climbed down again, leaning towards her with his hands on the kitchen table.

'I haven't had time to prepare supper yet. I had to call in at the hospital to see a patient and I've only just got back.'

He moved away towards the stove, reaching for a large cast-iron casserole.

'I'll do something quick and simple. How about an omelette and salad?'

'Lovely! Let me help.' Liz jumped up from the table.

'You can prepare the salad if you like while I do the omelette.'

Jacques lifted a round iron lid from the centre of the stove and inserted a poker. Liz watched as he vigorously stirred the glowing coals.

'This house feels like a real home,' she said, as she took the box of salad over to the sink. 'Do you live here all the time?'

Jacques began cracking eggs into a large earthenware bowl. 'I've got a room at the hospital where I stay when I have to. But whenever possible I get myself back here. This was where I grew up. My father was working every minute of the day and half the night and my grandmother was happy to have me here. My grandfather died only weeks after my mother. My grandmother said he never got over losing his precious daughter.'

'Your grandmother must have been sad to lose her daughter and her husband in such a short space of time.'

Jacques paused in his whisking of the eggs and looked across the kitchen at Liz. 'Yes, she was. But she was very resilient and she had to keep the family going. My mother had been the eldest child so there were her four teenage siblings still at home here. Then I came along to join them.'

'That must have been nice for you to have older children around you.'

'Oh, it was great fun for me to have young uncles and aunts to play with. But Grandmaman always told me I was special because I'd filled the space left by her daughter. She was like a mother to me. I called her Maman, not Grandmaman. She liked that.'

Liz felt a lump in her throat as she listened to Jacques talking about his childhood. For a poignant moment she could see the motherless boy running around this kitchen, dark hair flying, just like Melissa's. And, like Melissa, he would have been full of life, intent on living every moment to the full.

She brought herself out of her reverie as she carried the bowl of salad to the table and began to prepare a dressing of oil and vinegar mixed with fresh coriander and garlic.

'It sounds like you had a happy childhood in spite of the fact that you lost your mother,' Liz said gently.

Jacques placed the fluffy omelette on a huge, warm, blue-and-white serving plate.

'Everybody wanted me to be happy,' he said, the catch in his voice giving away his heightened emotions. 'I sometimes used to feel jealous that my older brothers and sisters and my aunts and uncles had known my mother, but my grandmother did all she could to take her place.'

He picked up the plate and placed it in the centre of the long wooden refectory table before drawing up a chair for Liz beside him. He waited, his hands resting on the back of her chair, until she was settled comfortably.

Liz sat quite still, breathing in the heady scent of Jacques's aftershave as he stood behind her. She could sense the warmth and friendly ambience of this room, which had seen so much life over the generations, wrapping around her.

'When my grandmother died,' Jacques said, serving some of the omelette on to Liz's plate, 'she left me this house. She always told me that was what she would do, because she knew I would be the only one who would want to live in it. It's a rambling old house, as you can see. Lovely in summer, but desperately cold in winter.'

'It's fabulous!' Liz said, savouring a mouthful of the fluffy omelette.

'The house or the omelette?'

Liz laughed. 'Both.'

'The omelette needs some black pepper.' Jacques lifted the tall pepper mill and ground pepper over Liz's omelette. 'More?'

'That's perfect, thank you.'

She took a sip of her wine. The delightful scent of the

excellent Bordeaux tantalised her nostrils even before the wine touched her lips.

'Excellent wine!'

'I'm glad you like it. I brought it up from the cellar earlier so that it could come up to room temperature. The cellar is very chilly, excellent for storing wine but you need a few hours before the wine becomes truly *chambré*.'

'Tell me, Jacques, didn't your brothers and sisters or your aunts and uncles want to have a share in this house?'

Jacques shook his head. 'They all preferred to have new houses, with all the modern conveniences. My grandmother had money in her own right from a legacy when she married my grandfather. She invested wisely so that she was able to leave money for each of her children and grandchildren to buy small modern houses. They didn't want the hassle of the upkeep of an old place like this. It's a constant financial drain, but I think it's worth spending time and money on.'

'Absolutely! But what happened to the house when you were working in Paris?'

A shadow crossed Jacques's face. 'Francine wanted me to sell it. She said there was no way she would ever come to live down here. But I insisted on keeping it. One of my uncles who lives in the village used to keep an eye on the place and he let me know if something needed repairing. I always knew I would come back here to live one day.'

Liz put down her fork and leaned against the back of her chair. 'But I thought you preferred the bright lights of Paris.'

A slow smile spread across his face. 'That's the image I sometimes like to portray. It was convenient to hang onto when I was trying to convince myself that I loved

Francine and the way of life we'd carved out for ourselves. Paris can be so exciting for a young man who'd only known the simple life in a sleepy area of the south.'

Liz remained quiet as Jacques paused, choosing his words carefully. She looked up at the candles, thinking how peaceful it was. There was a creaking sound over by the sink, probably the ancient pipes or one of the oak beams. Old houses seemed to have lives of their own. They'd absorbed so much living that they were able to give back some of what they'd taken away. And everybody who listened quietly could become a part of the past. Listening to Jacques talking now was giving her an insight into what he was really like. Her ideas about him were changing.

Jacques cleared his throat as his voice became husky. 'It was fun at first, living the high life in Paris—theatres, restaurants, travelling whenever I could get away from the hospital. But I began to realise that Francine and I had drifted into a relationship that simply wasn't working.'

'So you drifted out of it before it was too late.'

'Something like that. Meeting someone else helped me to make up my mind.'

'*Moi aussi*...me, too,' she said softly.

Jacques leaned forward and caressed the side of her face with his fingers. She felt delicious anticipation running through her.

He stood up, drawing her to her feet, holding her closely against him as his lips claimed hers.

She could feel her whole body beginning to tremble with the passion she'd been deliberately suppressing ever since they'd held each other earlier.

Jacques drew himself away, looking down at her with an infinitely tender expression.

'Elisabeth?' he queried huskily.

Liz knew exactly what he was asking and why he was holding off. 'Jacques, I want to make love with you,' she whispered. 'More than anything in the world.'

He breathed a deep sigh as he kissed her once more, this time with increasing passion. As his kiss deepened she felt the seductive power of his body claiming hers. Breathlessly, she moved in his arms, leaning back against the table as she tried to catch her breath.

Gently but swiftly, he disengaged her and swooped her up into his arms.

'It's time I showed you the rest of the house,' he said, smiling down at her as she snuggled against his chest. 'Shall we start with the master bedroom?'

'Mmm…' Liz was incapable of a coherent reply.

Lying back amid the rumpled sheets, Liz realised that she remembered very little of how she'd actually got into this enormous bed. Jacques had carried her up a wide staircase. They'd paused several times on the stairs for deep languorous kisses. At one point as they'd turned the corner of the staircase there had been a wide section of carpet where they'd started to make love.

Yes, she remembered quite a lot now! All of it ecstatically wonderful. The few items of clothing that had remained when they'd actually arrived in this enormous master bedroom had soon been discarded in the feverish rush to claim each other.

Liz looked up at the tapestry canopy above the bed, held in place with an ornate velvet ribbon above a mountain of squashy, down-filled pillows. This was the sort of room you saw in magazines about country houses. Slightly shabby in places, endless repairs and refurbishment always waiting to be done… She could see a damp patch above the window. But what a joy to live in a place like this!

She moved her head on the pillow so that she could look at the sleeping figure beside her. Jacques's hair had fallen down over his forehead in a tousled black mass. Asleep, he had the same innocent expression that Melissa wore.

They were so alike! She felt an outpouring of sheer love and had to restrain herself from kissing him awake again. He needed his sleep. Tomorrow…or rather today…he would be in the operating theatre again and she owed it to his patients to make sure that he wasn't tired.

Well, not too tired! She remembered how they'd wakened during the night and reached for each other time after time. She'd thought that their first night together had been wonderful, but this time she'd been in heaven. Still was! Her whole body tingled with the aftermath of their love-making.

She climbed out of bed and tiptoed over the wooden floor towards the window. There was a fur rug in front of the long casement window. She buried her toes in its soft pile as she peeped out through the curtains. The sun was rising over the top of the hill at the far end of the shore. A fisherman was sitting out there in the bay motionless on the smooth water as he waited to pull in his net.

She tightened the belt of the robe that she'd found on a nearby chair. Opening the window, she went out onto the balcony. The birds in the garden below were beginning to waken. A blackbird had something in its beak…a worm perhaps? She couldn't see from this distance. One of its noisy chicks, feathers fluffed out so that it appeared bigger than its mother, was hopping nearby, vociferously nagging its mother to give it some of the food.

'Come back to bed, Elisabeth.'

Liz turned at the sound of Jacques's voice. She went back into the room. After the chill of the early morning outside, the room felt warm and cosy. She sat on the edge of the bed, looking down lovingly at Jacques.

'I was watching the birds. You've got a beautiful garden.'

'We'll have breakfast in the garden. But first…'

He was reaching for her, his eyes registering tenderness and a deep, hungry, renewed desire.

'Jacques, I have to go. I promised Melissa I would be home for breakfast.'

He gave a resigned sigh as he leaned back against his pillows. 'I'm glad we had this one night together.'

A shiver of fear ran through her as she listened to his words. Was that all it had been? Another one-night stand, as Gina had so crudely phrased it? Had Jacques guessed that Melissa was his and he didn't want to take on the responsibility of a child?

She leaned across the bed and kissed him lightly on the lips. He made a gentle attempt to hold her but she wriggled free.

'I must go, Jacques. Melissa will be waiting.'

Jacques drew in his breath as he thought about the child who might possibly be his if some miracle had happened and his condition had reversed itself. Did Elisabeth suspect that Melissa might be his? If so, why hadn't she told him? Was it because she believed he didn't want children or a committed relationship? Yes, that was probably the reason. But until he'd had a medical examination it would be futile to speculate.

'When you're ready to go, I'll see you to the front door, Elisabeth,' Jacques said quietly.

'Thanks.' She smiled. 'It's possible I could get lost in this big rambling house.'

'Quite possible. We never did finish the grand tour last night.'

She turned at the door to the bathroom. Jacques was smiling again. She felt her spirits lifting.

'Next time I'll take you round the entire house,' he said.

'I'd like that,' Liz said, as she went into the bathroom.

Closing the door behind her, she realised that she would like it very much. But what she liked most was the fact that Jacques had said 'next time' just when she'd been having a few moments of panic.

Nothing had been resolved during their idyllic night together. They were still living in a fantasy world that only existed for the two of them. All other considerations were an encumbrance that would somehow have to be sorted out.

But not yet! She slipped into the scented foamy water of the huge bath with its brass claw legs. The bath was in the centre of the large bathroom. She lay in the foam, half hoping that Jacques would come in. When he didn't she told herself it was all for the best. She had to get a move on and return home with the breakfast croissants. She had to come down from cloud nine and return to the real world.

CHAPTER SIX

AS JACQUES scrubbed up in the anteroom of the operating theatre he was thinking about the consultation he'd arranged for that afternoon. It was unfortunate that the fertility specialist could only take him today. He had several operations to perform during the long morning ahead of him and he wouldn't have time for a break before leaving the hospital. But if he turned down this appointment, it was going to be several weeks before he could get another one and he didn't want to hold off any longer.

'You're looking very serious.'

Jacques put on a deliberately bright smile as Elisabeth joined him at the next sink to scrub up.

'I'm just reviewing the surgical procedure I'm going to use on our patient. It's rather an intricate operation.'

Liz continued to scrub. 'Yes, would you remind me exactly what you intend to do, Jacques? We've discussed it at length, I know, but just give me the salient points.'

Jacques turned off his tap with the crook of his elbow and held out his hands towards the scrub nurse who was standing by to assist him.

'As you know, we used to inject gentamicin directly into the nerve endings of the middle ear. This wasn't always successful because we couldn't gauge how much of the drug we were introducing. Too much gentamicin would be dangerous to the inner ear, too little would be ineffective. So I'm going to fix a catheter with a bulbous tip inside the eardrum. With that in place, we'll be able to control the concentration of the drug more strategically and our patient should be able to return to a more normal life as soon as possible.'

'Claude told me yesterday he was looking forward to being normal again. Life hasn't been easy for him recently. He has high hopes for this operation.'

'So have I! That's why I can't afford to make a mistake.'

'Jacques, you won't make a mistake.'

Mon dieu, how beautiful Elisabeth looked this morning! Her face was flushed and vivacious, probably from rushing around at home with her delightful but mischievous daughter. He'd seen so little of Elisabeth in the last few days since they'd spent that incredible night together.

He missed her so much but until he knew the outcome of the tests he was going to undertake he felt he had no right to try to make any progress with their relationship. As things stood at the moment with regard to his sterility, he hadn't been able to contemplate the startling possibility that Melissa might be his child. It would be a miracle!

He wondered, as he had done over and over again, if Elisabeth suspected that Melissa might be his child. After all, she didn't know he was supposedly sterile. Why hadn't she told him about her suspicions if indeed that was what she'd been thinking? The only conclusion he could draw was that she believed his story about not wanting a family of his own or a committed relationship. That would put her off confiding in him, wouldn't it?

In reality, he had no idea what Liz thought about the situation and he didn't want to spoil the relationship they had by questions that might threaten the fragile rapport that existed between them. Once more he reminded himself that until he'd had his medical examination everything regarding Melissa was pure speculation.

But he knew he had to put his own personal problems

to one side as he contemplated the operation he was about to perform. Elisabeth was looking up at him enquiringly, wondering no doubt why he was hesitating.

'Everybody makes mistakes,' he said quietly. 'I'm only human. But I'm going to do my level best to improve the quality of life for Claude. I'd like to see him happy again. Patients with Ménière's disease have a tough time.'

'Claude is one of the lucky ones. We got the diagnosis correct and now he's having an expert surgeon eradicate the condition.'

'Thanks for that boost to my confidence,' Jacques said.

The nurse standing close by moved forward to help Jacques into a sterile gown. He stood quite still until he was gowned and masked. Beside him, Liz was being helped by a second nurse.

As the two nurses stepped back, declaring the surgeon and his assistant to be ready for Theatre, Jacques smiled down at Liz, the eyes above the mask glittering with the excitement he always felt at the start of a long session in Theatre, however apprehensive he felt.

'Let's go, Dr Elisabeth.'

The anaesthetised patient was lying motionless on the operating table. There was no way of telling it was the lively, interesting Claude, Liz thought as she moved aside the dressing sheet to reveal the operating area around the ear.

The anaesthetist at the head of the table adjusted the flow of the cylinder by his side before nodding at Jacques to say that all was well.

As soon as she handed Jacques the first surgical instrument, Liz forgot she was nervous. Yes, there was a lot at stake but Jacques was extremely competent and experienced. He'd done this operation before and he would make a success of it if anybody could.

It took less time than she'd thought to place the bulbous-tipped catheter inside the eardrum, next to the inner ear. Jacques then administered the first injection of gentamicin through the catheter.

'That will start the healing process,' he said quietly, as he adjusted the flow of the drug. 'We should get good results as soon as the course of the disease is arrested.'

Liz went out to the anteroom as Claude was wheeled into the recovery room. She felt a sense of anticlimax now that her patient was no longer in her care. The medical staff would take over his new treatment. She would go up to the ward later to see how Claude was feeling after his recovery period but meanwhile she had to get back to A and E.

She peeled off her gown and tossed it in the laundry bin.

'Just a moment, Liz.'

She turned as Jacques came through the swing doors. 'Yes, Jacques. What can I do for you?'

Jacques pulled down his mask. 'Thanks for your help.'

'It was an interesting operation. I was glad to assist. I don't get to do much surgery these days.'

She waited. Jacques looked as if he had something important to say. She found she was holding her breath.

'Are you free on Sunday?'

She gave a relieved smile. An easy enough question to answer. 'Yes, I think so. What did you have in mind?'

'I thought you might like to come for lunch,' Jacques said. 'I want to show you I can cook other things beside omelettes. And I thought you would like to see more of the house. We didn't get past the kitchen and the master bedroom last Sunday.'

He was looking down at her with such an intense yet casually rakish expression. She could feel a certain sensuality simply oozing from him, in spite of the camouflage of his amorphous theatre gown.

She knew she was blushing as the memories flooded back. 'Yes, I'd love to see the whole house, but I'd better check what the rest of my family is up to on Sunday.'

'Do, please, bring Melissa,' Jacques said quickly.

'You might have to put your favourite antiques up on high shelves,' Liz said wryly.

'I'll ensure the place is totally childproof so long as I have a definite yes for Sunday.'

Liz smiled. 'We'll be there.'

The next patient was being wheeled into the operating theatre. Jacques nodded to Theatre Sister who was holding open the swing doors for his return.

'I'm on my way, Sister.'

Catherine emerged from one of the cubicles as Liz returned to A and E.

'Could you examine this patient, Elisabeth? She says she thinks she's had too much sun.'

Sister lowered her voice. 'There should be a sign on the beach advising people to sit in the shade more during August. That's the third case of sunburn this week.'

Liz went into the cubicle and smiled down at the patient who was lying on the examination couch. Looking down at her with critical eyes, Liz thought that she didn't seem to have had too much sun on her face. It was red, but not excessively so.

'I've been using a high-factor sunblock, Doctor,' the young woman said in a defensive tone before Liz could ask her.

'Let me take a few notes about you,' Liz said. 'My name's Elisabeth and you are…?'

'Monique. This is my boyfriend, Guillaume.'

Liz smiled at the young couple. Guillaume stood up from his chair and shook hands with Liz.

'Monique is in awful pain, Doctor. Can you give her something to help? You should see the burns on her body.'

'Would you like to undo your blouse, Monique, and the top of your shorts? That's the way….'

Liz bent closer to get a better look at the affected area. There were red patches around the side of Monique's body that were turning into a rash over her abdomen. Liz traced her finger over the line of the patches from the side of the body to the front.

She straightened up as the diagnosis became obvious to her.

'Typically following the path of the nerve,' she muttered under her breath, quoting from the textbook she'd practically memorised as a young medical student when she'd first learned about this condition.

'What was that?' Guillaume asked, leaning forward.

'Monique isn't suffering from sunburn. She's got shingles.'

The young man looked startled. 'Shingles! I've heard of it but what is it?'

'The medical name for this condition is herpes zoster. It's caused by the varicella-zoster virus that causes chickenpox.'

'I had chickenpox when I was a child,' Monique said, raising herself on her elbows to stare down at the rash that was forming on her torso.

Liz nodded. 'That's usually the case with shingles. The virus will have lain dormant in the nerve ganglia, that's like a junction box between the nerves. Something must have triggered it into being active again. Sunbathing can do that in some people. In other cases it's simply because the patient is run down.'

The young woman was looking anxious. 'Can you cure it, Doctor?'

Liz nodded. 'We can certainly help to relieve the symptoms and then let nature take its course. When did you first notice the red patches and the pain?'

'This morning.'

'Good. We've caught it early enough. If left untreated, shingles can take a long time to disappear. But if we catch it within the first three days we can shorten the time. I'm going to give you an antiviral drug which will certainly shorten the course of the disease.'

'Will you be keeping Monique in hospital?'

'No, no,' Liz assured the anxious young man. 'But she'll need plenty of rest. And she mustn't go out in the sun until she's completely clear.'

Guillaume smiled. 'Don't worry, I'll take good care of her. Thanks a lot, Doctor.'

There were other patients to treat. Liz was busy until mid-afternoon when she made a brief visit to the medical ward to check on Claude. He was lying very still with his eyes closed.

'How are you feeling now, Claude?' Liz asked, sitting down on the side of the bed.

'I'm OK. Can't hear very well, so I hope you've brought an ear trumpet with you, Elisabeth.'

Liz smiled. Claude was always outwardly cheerful, even when she could tell he was depressed.

'The hearing will return,' she reassured him. 'It's merely a reaction to the surgery. Meanwhile, we'll keep on treating your ear with gentamicin while we wait to see some results. It's going to be a while before the drug takes effect and you're completely cured.'

Claude nodded. 'I know. Is Jacques going to come in to see me?'

'Hasn't he been in?' Liz asked, surprised. 'Perhaps he's still in Theatre.'

'No, Sister said he'd taken a half-day off duty. I thought you might know if he's coming back into hospital this evening.'

'No, sorry, I've no idea where he is. He might have looked in on you while you came round from the anaesthetic.'

Claude smiled. 'Yes, that's probably what happened. Two senior doctors have been in to see me, one from the surgical team and one from the medical firm, I believe. I just wanted to have a chat with Jacques, that's all.'

'Well, is there something worrying you that I could help with?' Liz asked.

'Not really.' Claude looked unsure. 'My wife looked in this morning while I was still groggy. She's getting impatient with the time it's taking for me to get well. Marie's convinced herself it's got to be more than something wrong with the ear. She kept on saying, just before I came into hospital, that I've changed so much in the past year that—' He broke off, his voice choking with emotion.

Liz put her hand over Claude's as she tried to comfort him. She knew how he hated to seem weak, but he was struggling now to keep in control of himself. She would get in contact with Jacques—he would know how to handle the situation. Claude, understandably, didn't want to confide in a woman and she wasn't going to pry, wasn't going to dent his pride. It was obvious that Claude's relationship with his wife was going through a rocky patch.

'It's understandable that Marie should be worried about you when she doesn't fully understand the nature of your illness,' Liz said carefully. 'I'm sure that once your health begins to improve—as it will—your wife will be reassured.'

'I hope so,' Claude said. 'Marie is very highly strung and she jumps quickly to conclusions. Then the next minute she thinks of something else to worry about. I love her dearly, and I just want to get better and go home to her.'

Liz squeezed Claude's hand. 'You will, Claude, you will. You'll make good progress because you've got a very positive attitude. I've dealt with a lot of patients and it's always the ones with positive attitudes who can speed up their recovery.'

She stayed for as long as she felt she could be spared from A and E. As she left, Claude thanked her for being so understanding.

'I wish I could do more,' she said.

She and Jacques knew how to cure the physical part of his problem. Hopefully this would help towards solving the emotional aspect.

As she was leaving the ward, Liz found herself wondering where Jacques had gone to. It was strange he hadn't told her he had a free afternoon. They had become much closer. She felt it was only a matter of time before she dared broach the subject that was uppermost on her mind.

Over at the private fertility clinic, Jacques was feeling nervous. It had been a long drive down the coast. He hadn't wanted to confide in any of his colleagues so he'd simply looked in one of the medical magazines that he regularly took to keep him updated in the general world of medicine and surgery outside his own field.

'Jacques Chenon?'

The young nurse-receptionist smiled as she held open the door to the consulting room. The tall, middle-aged man with greying hair sitting at the desk stood up and held out his hand as the door was closed. Jacques looked around him at the opulent furniture, the soft lights, the muted shade of the deep-pile carpet that muffled the sound of his feet as he advanced nervously towards the desk to shake the consultant's hand.

No escape now! He could imagine just how daunting it would be for a young man, desperate to have a family, to be ushered in here to confess that he'd been trying for months to get his wife pregnant but…

'Do sit down, Monsieur Chenon.'

The tall man waved a hand towards the large leather chairs in a sitting area over by the window. He picked up the case notes before walking over to join Jacques.

There was an initial conversation about the hot weather, both men agreeing that it was only to be expected in August near to the Mediterranean coast. The specialist hoped that the journey hadn't been too arduous and that Jacques had found his clinic, tucked away in the low hills behind the sea, not too difficult to access from the coastal road.

Rather than putting Jacques at his ease, this small talk was only increasing his feeling that it had been a mistake to come here. Why hadn't he left things as they were? He and Elisabeth were getting on so well now. It would be a pity for either of them to spoil the situation.

'So, tell me what the problem is, Jacques.'

Looking now at the consultant's direct gaze, Jacques knew that the ice-breaking part of the consultation was over. He tried a similar technique himself when he was treating nervous patients. But now it was time to get down to the nitty-gritty.

'It's like this, Dr Fromentin…'

'Please, call me Henri. I find it puts my patients at ease if they call me by my first name.'

Jacques found himself relaxing. 'So do I.' He hesitated. 'I work at the new hospital in St Gabriel. The Clinique de la Côte.'

Henri Fromentin smiled. 'Jacques Chenon—of course! Head of Surgery there, aren't you? We spoke on the phone some weeks ago when I referred a patient to you.'

Jacques sighed. 'Initially I thought of trying to keep my identity a secret but just now I thought…well, as a dear friend of mine sometimes says in English, "What the hell!"'

Henri laughed. 'He or she must be an interesting character.'

'She's actually half-French. A woman who's very dear to me. That's why I'm here.'

Jacques paused. He was saying far more than he'd meant to. Henri Fromentin had that effect on people.

The fertility specialist leaned towards Jacques. 'Whatever you're going to say, Jacques, is all in the strictest confidence. Believe me, I've heard it all before, many times. There's nothing new under the sun where human beings are concerned. I'm guessing that you've come here because you and the charming half-French, half-English lady are hoping for a family and—'

'Quite the reverse, Henri. My French-English lady has a delightful daughter aged four. The timing of the child's conception seems to coincide with a particularly amorous night we spent together. Neither of us was free at the time to pursue a relationship. Which may be why my friend is loath to inform me that it's possible I might be the father of her daughter.'

'Congratulations! But how can I...?'

'The problem is that I've been sterile since a particularly severe bout of mumps at the age of twenty.'

Henri frowned. 'Ah, I see. And how old are you now?'

'Thirty-nine. The lady in question is twenty-nine. She was, at the time, married to someone else but she divorced soon after our liaison.'

'Ah!' Henri repeated as he leaned back in his chair, placing the tips of his fingers together, appearing to be deep in thought.

'Did your friend...? Look, can we give her a name, do you think? It's all in the strictest confidence.'

'Elisabeth. She's a colleague of mine. But, please, don't write that down.'

Henri put the case notes down on a small table beside his chair. 'It's all in my head but not recorded. I was going to ask if Elisabeth had gone back to her husband after the two of you made love.'

Jacques frowned. 'I don't know. I hope not.'

Henri's expression brightened. 'So, does that mean you would be happy if this child was yours?'

'I would be ecstatic! I've always wanted children. I've had to pretend ever since I was twenty that I didn't want a family of my own, that children would interfere with my life.'

Jacques broke off and stared at Henri. 'I've never admitted that to anyone. Not even to my father, who so often told me he wanted me to have children. I always—'

'It's a perfectly normal reaction,' Henri said. 'Other sterile patients have told me this. Now, have you had a sperm test since you were twenty?'

Jacques shook his head. 'It's not something you relish,

being told that you're abnormal, that you're not manly enough to father a child.'

'Jacques, you as a doctor should know that it's got nothing to do with being manly. You had mumps. Your sperm count went down.'

'Two consultants told me my sperm count was zero,' Jacques said quietly.

'Jacques, that was nineteen years ago. Now, have you had a relationship with a woman for any length of time?'

Jacques nodded. 'For two years I lived with someone in Paris. My partner was a model. Before we got engaged and she moved in with me, I told her I couldn't father children and she said that was a relief. She said she'd never wanted a family. Children would ruin her figure and spoil our hedonistic lifestyle, which was pretty hectic at the time.'

'So you took her at her word and had sex without any form of contraception for two years?'

'Exactly. And Francine didn't conceive. So...'

Henri raised an eyebrow. 'Jacques, isn't there a possibility that Francine might have been on the Pill? A woman who needs a good figure for her professional life doesn't take any chances.'

Jacques swallowed hard. 'It's possible. She was a very secretive sort of woman....'

Henri nodded understandingly. 'I think we'd better assess your sperm count, don't you? If you'd like to go into my examination cubicle and produce a specimen for testing, we'll take it from there.'

Jacques could feel himself freezing with embarrassment at the thought of producing a specimen in such a clinical situation.

'I'm not sure if I can....'

Henri put a hand on his arm. 'Don't worry, Jacques.

That's what all my patients think. You'll find everything you need in there. Take your time. There's no hurry. No one will interrupt you. I'm going off to see another patient now. Just press the bell for one of the nurses to take away your specimen when you're ready.'

Jacques could feel himself relaxing again. 'Just one more thing, Henri. When will you be able to give me the result of my test?'

Henri looked thoughtful. 'Oh, quite quickly actually.'

Jacques leaned forward. 'By Sunday?'

Henri smiled knowingly. 'Sunday is going to be an important day, is it?'

Jacques nodded.

'I hope for your sake the results are favourable. If not…' Henri spread his hands in front of him. 'There's no need to live without a family nowadays if you really want one.'

'I haven't looked that far ahead,' Jacques said. 'One step at a time. I would just like to claim this child as my own. She's already very dear to my heart.'

Driving back along the coast road, Jacques remembered that he must call in to see Claude. His patient would think he'd deserted him. He'd looked in while Claude had still been under the after effects of the anaesthetic and he'd arranged for his colleagues to keep an eye on him.

His mobile phone rang. Jacques pulled over onto the grass verge to take the call.

'Jacques, where are you?'

His spirits lifted as he heard Elisabeth's voice. 'I'm on my way back to hospital. I had to see a medical colleague about a patient.'

'Your mobile's been switched off for ages.'

'I was officially off duty. Is there a problem I should know about?'

'I'm worried about Claude…oh, not his physical condition. He's doing very well at the moment, but he's depressed. That wife of his is being so unhelpful.'

'I was going to go and see him on the ward anyway, but I'll make him my first priority. Elisabeth, how are you? You sound a bit fraught.'

'Oh, I'm just tired, that's all. Been working all day and…' Liz hesitated. 'I didn't know where you were. Nobody here in hospital did either.'

'Elisabeth, my duties are all covered by my colleagues. I was officially off duty. What's the problem?'

At the other end of the phone, Liz was sitting in the sister's office. She had just finished suturing a deep cut in a little boy's arm. The child had gone out looking pleased with himself because Dr Elisabeth had put a nice rainbow-coloured bandage over the top of his stitches.

But after her patient had gone, a feeling of exhaustion had suddenly hit her and she knew she had to try once more to see if Jacques was answering his phone.

Listening to Jacques's voice, she realised that she was overreacting. She had no right to try to keep tabs on Jacques. He was completely free to come and go as he pleased.

'There isn't a problem, Jacques,' she said quietly. 'Look, I've got to go. One more patient to see and then I'm going off duty. See you tomorrow.'

Jacques looked out of the car window at the waves pounding on the shore near the coast road. A strong wind had blown up during the afternoon and the trees were bowing down under the strain of withholding the force of it. Clouds had obscured the sun. There would be a storm before night fell. Out at sea he could see the white flecks on the tops of the high waves.

He leaned back against his seat. If only he'd been able to confide in Elisabeth! She'd sounded worried about him. And he was worried about her! The two of them should get together and have a heart to heart tonight. Clear the air. Too many secrets made it impossible to have an honest relationship.

He picked up his mobile again. But even as the idea came to him, he dismissed it as being totally impracticable. Wonderful as it would have been to spend the evening with Elisabeth, he didn't want a heart to heart until he knew whether there was the remotest chance that he was the father of her child. If they discussed it now, they would simply be stumbling about in the dark.

Liz hung up and picked up her stethoscope from the desk. Jacques had sounded decidedly defensive on the phone. He was hiding something. But so was she!

The sooner they both came clean, the better!

She slung her stethoscope around her neck and went out of the office, heading for her next patient. She pushed her own worries aside as she smiled down at the worried-looking patient.

'Now, tell me what happened to you,' she said in a sympathetic tone as she reached for the elderly lady's hand.

CHAPTER SEVEN

LIZ was barely awake as she reached for the phone.

'Jacques!' Her voice came out in a surprised early morning croak.

'Did I waken you, Elisabeth?'

'Well, it is Sunday morning.' She adjusted her pillows with one hand and leaned back to take a sip of water from the glass beside her bed. 'Are you still expecting us for lunch?'

'Well, yes and no.'

Liz could feel her spirits drooping. Oh, no! But, then, this wasn't entirely unexpected this week. First Jacques had disappeared for a whole afternoon with his mobile switched off and now he'd called to cancel their Sunday lunch together.

'It's rather difficult for me to discuss it over the phone, Elisabeth. That's why I'm calling you early before the rest of your family get up.'

There was a pause. Liz waited for Jacques to elaborate. 'Jacques, are you still there?'

'Yes, I'm just thinking how to put this without upsetting you. You see, the fact of the matter is I think it would be better if you didn't bring Melissa with you today.'

Liz took a deep breath. 'I see.'

'I don't think you do.'

'Oh, yes, I've got the picture, Jacques.'

Yes, she could see quite clearly how Jacques was thinking. He'd been pretending all along that he welcomed Melissa. He'd had Liz fooled completely when he'd played with Melissa on the shore of the little cove. He'd seemed to enjoy teaching her how to steer the boat. The perfect family man! But in reality he was still the man who'd told her he didn't want children of his own because they would be a threat to his lifestyle.

'Elisabeth, I hope Melissa won't be disappointed.'

'Well, you're in luck there because I haven't yet told her she was supposed to be going to have lunch at your house, Jacques. She gets very excited when there's a treat in store so it makes it easier for everybody if I spring things on her as a surprise. At four years old children are very vulnerable and easily hurt.'

'I really am sorry, Elisabeth. But you'll understand when you come here today that—'

'Jacques, I'm not sure if I can make it without Melissa. My mother and sister have their own lives to lead, you know.'

'Please, try, Elisabeth. We need to talk. And we can't have a proper discussion if Melissa is around.'

Liz swallowed hard. Jacques sounded uncharacteristically solemn. This was a serious talk he was planning. This was going to be the high peak of their relationship when they both confessed all. It was make-or-break time.

And after that...? Would it be all downhill?

'I'll try to come. I'll call you later this morning.'

She cut the connection and swung her legs over the side of the bed. The summer-weight duvet was half on the floor. It had been another hot night. The storms of the last few days had failed to lower the temperature and it had been difficult to sleep. Even more difficult when you were worried about how you were going to keep going with a relationship that was proving more and more impossible.

She went over to her tiny shower cubicle and let the warm water cascade over her as she tried to clear her thoughts. In her heart of hearts she knew, with the benefit of hindsight, that it would have been better to have come clean with Jacques from the very beginning. But she'd been so afraid of losing him. If she'd sprung the truth on him early on, they wouldn't have had this brief period of happiness together.

She reached for a towel and patted herself dry. Emerging from the shower, she was just in time to hear someone knocking on her bedroom door.

'Maman! What a lovely surprise!' Liz was pulling on her robe as she opened the door. 'You're not usually awake so early, especially on Sunday.'

Karine smiled as she walked over to sit down on the cushioned window-seat. 'I heard you in the shower, Elisabeth, and I thought I'd drop in for a chat. I couldn't sleep last night. It was so hot, wasn't it?'

As Liz sat down on her bed and smiled across at her mother by the window, she was thinking how attractive she was for a woman of her age. She'd kept her figure and she was always impeccably dressed. The cosmetic work she'd had done at the dentist recently had restored her beautiful smile.

'You look good in that silk robe, Maman. Red suits you.'

'Thank you, darling.' Karine hesitated. 'I lay awake worrying last night.'

Liz felt a pang of anxiety. 'Anything I can do?'

Karine gave her daughter a brilliant smile. 'No, basically I'm fine. You and Gina are so good to me. But I sometimes wonder if you're devoting too much of your lives to taking care of me. I don't want to cramp your style.'

'Mum, you take care of yourself!'

Unconsciously, Liz had broken into English. When she'd been very small and she'd lived in England with her parents, that had been the language they'd all spoken together and she still regarded it as her first language.

'Gina and I love living here in France with you.'

'I know you love living in France, but you would tell me if you wanted to move out of the house, wouldn't you, Elisabeth?'

'Of course I would, but I don't.'

Liz paused as she wondered why her mother was looking at her like that. As if she was expecting some important revelation.

'Mum, I'm happy here, but…'

Liz had been planning to tell her mother the truth. She owed it to her to stop all this secrecy in the house. In spite of Gina's concerns, Liz knew that, from a medical point of view, her mother was now strong and healthy enough to take it.

She took a deep breath. 'Actually, I do need to talk to you about something that's worrying me.'

Karine smiled. 'I thought you might say that. Actually, I came in here while everybody was asleep, hoping for a heart to heart. I'm not worried about myself but I am worried about you, Elisabeth. You can't carry that secret around much longer, can you?'

Liz jumped up from the bed and crossed the room to sit beside her mother.

'Is it so obvious, Mum?'

Karine nodded. 'Ever since you came back to France. Elisabeth, I've always known that Mike couldn't possibly be Melissa's father.'

Liz swallowed hard. 'You've been talking to Gina?'

Karine leaned forward and squeezed her daughter's

hand reassuringly. 'No, of course I haven't. If I'd wanted to discuss it with Gina I'd have taken her on one side five years ago when you were recovering from your night out with Jacques Chenon.'

Liz could feel the blood draining from her face. 'You knew?'

'Of course I knew, darling,' Karine said, gently. 'I may be over the hill in your eyes but I know when somebody has fallen head over heels in love. I knew you weren't going to go back to Mike, thank goodness! And you weren't the sort of girl who would sleep around with somebody who wasn't going to play an important part in your life.'

'But why didn't you say something to me?'

'Because…because it wasn't my place to interfere. I've always believed that a mother should wait until her children ask for their advice. My own mother was too inquisitive. Too quick to try to impose her ideas on me. She didn't want me to marry your father. She said he was too old and set in his ways for me. And that made me all the more determined that I would do it my way.'

Liz leaned forward. 'Oh, Mum! I'm glad you did go your own way. I had the most fantastic father a girl could ever wish for and you and Daddy always seemed so happy together.'

'We were. I had a wonderful life with your father.' Karine paused. 'So when I saw that you were determined to go your own way, I didn't ask any questions. I knew you would tell me in your own time.'

'But how did you know I'd been out with Jacques that night five years ago?'

'St Gabriel is a small community, Elisabeth. One of my friends happened to be in the restaurant having dinner at a nearby table. She told me that the handsome son of the owner had spent a great deal of time talking to my daughter. I knew you stayed out all night and came back looking radiantly happy. When you told me you were pregnant a couple of months later…well, I just put two and two together.'

'And you're not shocked?'

'Shocked?' Karine gave her characteristically charming, tinkling laugh. 'Darling, I'm completely unshockable! I enjoyed a decidedly misspent youth in Paris. I think one reason why my own mother tried to put me off marrying your father was because she thought I would never settle down with an older man. She was holding her breath until she was reassured that the marriage was going to last. And just before she died, she told me I'd been right and she was sorry she'd tried to interfere.'

'Oh, Mum, it's so good to talk to you, woman to woman. I was planning to tell you about Jacques being Melissa's father but I wanted to wait until I'd broken the news to him.'

Karine's eyes widened in astonishment. 'You mean Jacques doesn't know?'

'There were so many reasons why I couldn't tell him. We'd made a pact that we wouldn't contact each other. We both had other partners at the time. When we met up again I thought he would be married. But one of the most important reasons was that Jacques had told me he didn't want to have children and—'

'Didn't want to have children! What kind of a man is that?'

'Exactly! Mum, I just wanted a little breathing space with him before I told him the truth. When I break the news it's going to spoil everything, isn't it?'

Karine took a deep breath. 'Well, it's certainly not going to make things any easier, I agree.' She hesitated. 'I don't want to interfere…oh, heavens, I sound just like my mother…but you do have to tell him. And the sooner the better.'

'I have an inkling it's not going to be a total shock to him. Like me, I think Jacques has been biding his time. Waiting for the right moment to tell me he suspects that Melissa is his daughter. He phoned me a short while ago to ask me not to bring her with me when I go to his house today. He says he wants to have a serious discussion about something.'

'Good! It's time everything was out in the open. If Jacques Chenon doesn't want to shoulder his responsibilities…'

'Oh, he'll do that, Mum! Knowing the kind of man he is, he'll want to offer me a lifetime of support financially, but I'm afraid that it's going to change our relationship for ever. And that's why I've been holding off.'

'Darling, whatever happens today, you must be truthful. Tell Jacques how you feel. He might change into a caring father.'

'I don't want Jacques to change out of a sense of duty,' Liz said quietly. 'I don't want him to think I trapped him into an intolerable situation.'

'Well, you still have to give him the option,' Karine said slowly. 'Go along there today and be strong. Don't worry about Melissa. She'll be happy here with Gina and me. We love having her with us.'

'Thanks, Mum.' Liz leaned across and hugged her mother. 'I wish I'd talked to you sooner.'

Karine smiled. 'So do I. But maybe it was all for the best. Perhaps each generation is meant to keep secrets from their parents until they've sorted out the problems for themselves.'

* * *

Jacques opened the door while Liz was parking the car in the drive. She looked across at him and smiled as she walked up the front steps.

'You're looking lovely,' he said, drawing her towards him.

'Thank you.' Liz smoothed down the skirt of her stone-coloured linen dress. 'I'm usually in trousers when I'm off duty but I thought I'd make an effort today. It sounded as if we were going to have a very serious discussion so I thought I'd dress as if I were going to a conference.'

Jacques's eyes flickered. 'Well, I approve. Hope you don't mind if I stay in my jeans.'

'Not at all!'

Liz could feel that they were both nervous. The sooner they started the discussion the better.

As they walked into the house together, Jacques's mobile started ringing.

'Excuse me, Elisabeth.'

She watched as Jacques listened. He was frowning now. She began to go towards the kitchen but Jacques held her arm to detain her.

'Don't go. This concerns you,' he said, frowning as he cupped his hand over the phone for a few seconds.

'Yes, Francine,' he continued as if there had been no interruption. 'I'd hoped you would answer your messages sooner. You heard my question, didn't you? You understand what I'm getting at?'

Liz watched Jacques's face contorting with undisguised contempt as he listened to his ex-fiancée's voice.

'So for two years you deceived me?'

He was concentrating again as Francine talked rapidly. Liz had no idea what this was all about and was feeling decidedly embarrassed.

'Jacques, you can explain later,' Liz said as she pulled away and walked into the kitchen.

If Jacques wanted to have a row with his ex-girlfriend over the phone, she didn't want to have any part of it. She walked over to the ancient stove where a cafetière of coffee was coming to the boil.

Just in time! She grabbed a cloth because the handle was hot. Quickly, she removed the cafetière and poured out two cups.

Jacques had followed her into the kitchen, still continuing his heated exchange.

'But if I'd only known you were on the Pill, Francine!'

Liz sat down at the table and took a sip of her coffee. Why shouldn't Francine have been on the Pill if they lived together for two years? She felt nothing except a surge of jealousy that Francine should have lived with Jacques for so long before she herself knew him. She couldn't bear to think of him having a previous love life. But, then, she'd been married and that didn't stop her from feeling as if she and Jacques were young lovers experiencing true love for the first time whenever they were together.

Jacques was listening intently now as he sat down at the table close to Liz.

'But of course it would have made a difference to my life, Francine!'

Jacques took a deep breath to calm himself.

Liz placed a cup of coffee in front of him. Jacques took a sip as he continued to listen to a tirade of invective. Finally he spoke, this time in a calmer voice as if reasoning with a recalcitrant child.

'Francine, because you chose to deceive me I assumed I was sterile, but now…'

Liz stared at Jacques as the truth dawned on her.

Jacques had thought he couldn't possibly be Melissa's father! That was why he'd never questioned her.

She put a hand over his as she listened to his distraught voice. 'Why didn't you tell me you were on the Pill?'

Liz squeezed Jacques's hand. 'Tell me the truth,' she whispered. 'What...?'

'I've got to go, Francine. Yes, it might be all in the past to you but it affects my life now and in the future.'

Jacques cut the connection and turned towards Liz.

He took a deep breath. 'Elisabeth, did you sleep with your husband after we made love on the beach?'

The directness of the question and the ominous tone of his voice was completely unnerving. Liz's hand was shaking as she put her cup down in the saucer. Drops of coffee splattered on the wooden surface of the table. She turned anguished eyes towards his.

'No, of course I didn't! I think I'd already decided to divorce Mike when I went to the restaurant that night. Meeting you only made me more certain that I was doing the right thing. In spite of that, being still technically married, I felt guilty after we'd made love but—'

'I felt guilty, too.'

Jacques gave a deep sigh, toying with the spoon in his saucer, turning it in his hand, gripping it as if trying to get rid of the tormented feelings he'd suffered after the euphoria of his night with Elisabeth had evaporated.

'I still felt I wasn't free until I'd officially broken off our engagement and cancelled the wedding.'

He was looking down at Liz with troubled eyes. 'Why didn't you tell me about Melissa? I loved you so much. How could you have kept it secret that I was her father?'

Liz shivered as she heard Jacques using the past tense as if his love for her was already dead.

'Jacques—'

'Why didn't you tell me that Melissa was my daughter?'

Liz bridled at his accusatory tone. 'We'd promised not to contact each other, remember?'

Jacques spread his arms in an expansive curve. 'Yes, but something as momentous as the birth of a child is not something to keep to yourself.'

'Jacques! Don't, please, don't!'

Liz stood up and moved over to the window, staring out at the garden beyond. A blackbird was singing with carefree abandon. A couple of squirrels were chasing each other in the trees beyond the rough-hewn wooden gazebo. Where had her own happiness gone? Only minutes ago she'd been full of hope but now…

She turned and gazed at Jacques imploringly. 'You told me you didn't want to have children of your own. You outlined the carefree, hedonistic lifestyle that you and Francine had. You said that—'

'Yes, I know I did. It was all a pretence.'

She turned as he strode across the room to put his hands on her arms, holding her gently as he looked into her eyes.

'I can see how you would have been taken in,' he said. 'I'd been trying to play the same shallow, superficial character ever since I was twenty. Believe it or not, I first began the pretence on medical advice.'

'You were very convincing.'

'Was I?' Jacques relaxed his grip, moving to stand beside her, looking unseeingly out of the window. 'I wish I hadn't been. I wish you'd been able to see through me and tell me that…' He broke off, staring ahead of him as he realised the futility of trying to change the past.

Elisabeth turned back towards the window. Both she and Jacques looked as if they were contemplating the view of the lovely garden but each of them was racked with anguished thoughts. There was an uneasy silence as they waited to see who would continue the argument.

'It wasn't your fault that you took me at my word when I said I didn't want a family,' Jacques said. 'Most people believed what I said. Even my father, so it's unrealistic of me to think that you might have seen through me. The truth was, I was so sad I'd been diagnosed as sterile that the only way I could handle it was by pretending I didn't care.'

He turned to face her, his hand gently caressing her cheek. She stood stock still as she looked up into his tormented eyes.

'Jacques, what was the medical problem?' she asked softly.

'I had a very bad attack of mumps when I was twenty,' he said wearily. 'When I recovered, my doctors did various tests on me. They said my sperm count was zero. That I would never be a father.'

'Oh, Jacques, that must have been devastating! No wonder you reacted as you did!'

Jacques looked down at Elisabeth, feeling sorry that he'd spoken so harshly before. But the phone call from Francine had set his nerves on edge. He would be happy if he never saw Francine again in his life. But he couldn't bear to lose Elisabeth.

'Elisabeth, you are so understanding,' he said gently, as he leaned down and kissed her lightly on the lips.

She felt her body reacting but the contact was only momentary. It felt like a farewell kiss between two people who'd briefly been lovers but had decided to call it a day.

Liz took a deep breath. 'Jacques, have you had a sperm count recently?'

'I had one this week. That was why I took the afternoon off—to go to a fertility clinic down the coast. I got a full report from the specialist yesterday. I'm absolutely normal. The problem has resolved itself over the years.'

'Oh, Jacques, I'm so happy for you and for...' She stopped in mid-sentence. She'd been going to say 'for us' but that would have presumed that they were going to stay together. Seeing the expression on Jacques's face, she wasn't feeling optimistic.

'Let's walk in the garden,' Jacques said, taking her hand and leading her out through the kitchen door. 'We need a period of calm.'

They walked for a while in silence. Liz was frightened to speak until she had something to contribute that would help Jacques to see just how hard it had been for her, making and sticking to the decision to go it alone. The tension between them had eased but she knew that Jacques was still unhappy at being excluded from the first four years of his daughter's life.

'Jacques, it wasn't easy for me,' she began tentatively. 'I was in an impossible situation. After I'd made my decision I had to stick to it—surely you must see that?'

'I'm trying to see it from both sides,' he said. 'Trying to reason out what I would have done if I'd been in your shoes. But it doesn't alter the fact that I had a daughter out there who didn't know I was her father, who still doesn't know I'm her father....'

He put out his arm and drew her down beside him on a wooden seat.

Liz remained quite still, simply content that they were close to each other. Physically close, but emotionally miles apart. How could they resolve their differences? She'd known it wouldn't be easy when the truth came out but she hadn't imagined she could feel as helpless as she did at this moment.

She gazed ahead of her at the beautiful garden, trying to get herself in harmony with the natural surroundings. Trying so hard to gather strength from the external forces of nature around her. A dove was cooing to his mate at the top of one of the tall trees that formed a windbreak on the coastal side of the garden. The mate was fluffing out her wings, pretending she wasn't interested in being wooed.

Rather like herself! Pretending that the last thing she wanted was a reconciliation. Jacques was in a state of shock and it was up to her to take him out of himself so that they could start afresh.

From the other side of the tall trees she could hear the waves breaking on the shore. She turned to look at Jacques.

'Let's go and have a swim, Jacques. That will make us both feel better. We've both got something to celebrate. The fact that we're being truthful with each other at long last is a cause for celebration, don't you think?'

'Elisabeth, I can't forget that you actually returned to work with me at the Clinique and you didn't tell me that Melissa was mine! How could you keep a secret like that? A man has a right to know he's a father.'

'But I really believed that you didn't want to be a father! And then, after we were getting on so well together, I was playing for time. Trying to hold onto our fragile relationship for as long as possible before I told you and everything was spoilt.'

'Is everything spoilt now?' he asked quietly.

'No, it isn't! Because now I know that you're not the type of man you were pretending to be. You were pretending that you didn't want children of your own when all the time…'

'But it could have all been so different if you'd told me about Melissa when she was first born, or even when you were pregnant.' Jacques clasped his hands together and gave a deep sigh. 'As soon as you knew you were pregnant! That would have been so wonderful for me.'

He was shouting now as he realised what it would have been like to have experienced such sheer joy.

'To have known five years ago that I was no longer sterile! To realise that all my hopes and dreams were coming true!'

Liz leaned across and took one of his big hands in hers, gently stroking each finger as if he were a child.

'Jacques, we'd agreed not to contact each other ever again. I thought you would be married to Francine and… Look, we're going through a period of adjustment. We should simply be happy that we have a beautiful child. Let's stop all these recriminations and, as I often tell my patients, let nature take its course.'

She stood up, her face set as she came to a decision. 'Let's have a truce, Jacques. When we've decided what we want to do about the future, we'll talk again.'

Jacques stood up, drawing her into his arms, holding her close against him. 'I've already decided what I want in the future. What I want now. I'm angry, yes, I'm furious, but Melissa is my child and—'

Liz disengaged herself from his arms. 'I'm going home, Jacques. Let's end the discussion here. We're simply going round in circles.'

She walked with determined steps towards the drive. Her car keys were in her pocket. Jacques had become very quiet as he walked beside her, a look of resignation on his face.

'Perhaps it's for the best that you go,' he said quietly. 'I clearly need to come to terms with all of this.'

She nodded, putting the keys in the ignition. Jacques lowered his head towards the open window.

'Goodbye, Elisabeth.' He moved his hands from the car.

As Liz drove off, she felt as if her heart would break. She drove slowly along the coast road back towards St Gabriel. People were streaming out of the village church, tourists and villagers intermingling. Everybody happy to be out in the warm summer sunshine, looking forward to their Sunday lunch.

Jacques had put something to cook in the oven, she'd noticed as they'd had their tense discussion in the kitchen. The dish had smelt like lamb with rosemary. One of her favourites for Sunday lunch in France and in England. But she wasn't hungry any more.

She'd lost her appetite for life as well. If she and Jacques were to begin being parents with them both feeling hurt, there wasn't much hope for the future.

Perhaps it would be easier if she turned round, went back and told Jacques their affair was over. Over before it had really started. He could see Melissa as much as he liked but as far as she herself was concerned…

Liz pulled over to the side of the road as the tears rolled down her cheeks. There was a packet of tissues somewhere in the glove compartment. She rummaged amidst the clutter, pricking her finger on the edge of a steel nail file before dabbing her eyes and blowing her nose furiously.

As far as she was concerned, if she went back now to see Jacques she would simply fall into his arms and beg him to stop thinking about the past and start again as if they were still lovers without a care in the world. But somehow she didn't think that Jacques was ready for that—and she didn't know if he ever would be.

Jacques watched Liz heading down the drive towards the wrought-iron gates. He was still angry. He couldn't believe she could have kept the truth from him for so long.

He began to walk inside as Liz's car disappeared through the gates.

Yes, he could see that there were valid reasons why Liz had kept quiet. She had been married at the time of Melissa's conception and she'd felt guilty. She'd expected him to marry Francine. She'd also thought he didn't want to be a father…which made a big difference. And it had been entirely of his own doing. They'd also agreed not to contact each other.

He went into the kitchen, lifted out the lamb and switched off the oven. When it had cooled down he would put it in the fridge. He'd lost his appetite. What had been planned as a celebration had turned into a travesty.

He sat down and took a sip of his cold coffee. His anger was dissipating. Yes, he was beginning to see it from Elisabeth's point of view. Having agreed not to contact each other, then…

But finding herself pregnant with his child! A momentous experience like that. If only Elisabeth had known what a difference it would make to his life, she would have…

He leapt to his feet. All he knew was that he was missing Elisabeth already. He had no right to direct his frustrated anger towards her, it wasn't her fault. He wanted her with him now. And he wanted to see his daughter again. But after the way he'd behaved today, he wasn't sure if Elisabeth would want to see him again. It hadn't been a good start to their joint parenting.

He realised he was going round in circles again. Elisabeth had wanted to swim. If he'd calmed down and gone into the sea with her, they might have reconciled their differences there and then.

He would never know, he thought as he grabbed a towel and made for the beach, every fibre of his being longing to be close to Elisabeth again. A long strenuous swim should calm him down or at least make him too tired to think any more....

CHAPTER EIGHT

IT WAS only days since they'd had their showdown but Liz was feeling the strain of the cold war that existed between Jacques and herself. She'd hoped he might phone to ask if she would take Melissa to his house. For a man who professed to want children, he was being decidedly slow to claim his daughter.

'The results of the blood test you ordered on our last patient are here, Doctor,' the young nurse said, bringing in a sheaf of papers and placing them on the desk in the A and E office.

'Thanks, Béatrice. Are you going off duty now?'

The young nurse smiled. 'I'm going to that new disco down by the beach. Have you been there, Elisabeth?'

Liz smiled. 'No, I haven't got much time to myself in the evenings these days.'

'You've got a little girl, haven't you? I saw you with her on the beach one afternoon when you were off duty. She looks very pretty. I noticed her lovely long dark hair and—' Béatrice broke off as Jacques walked in.

'I'd better be off, Elisabeth.'

Béatrice liked their head of surgery but he'd been in a bit of a bad mood for the past few days. All the nurses had noticed it. Not a bit like he usually was, he'd been snapping at her and her colleagues if they didn't come up to scratch. And his mouth was constantly set in that hard line.

Jacques closed the door behind the young nurse and went over to the desk with determined strides.

'Talking of Melissa's lovely long dark hair, I can't believe it took me so long to realise that—'

'Oh, Jacques, please, don't start this again. I couldn't—'

'I was only going to ask when I'm going to see my daughter again.'

He leaned against the edge of the desk.

'Jacques, we haven't decided what we're going to say to her, have we? And until we can be civil to each other again—'

'I'm perfectly civil! I've hardly spoken to you in days so how you can accuse me of being uncivil, I don't know.'

Jacques relented. 'I'm sorry, I shouldn't have spoken to you like that but I hadn't realised how deeply learning that Melissa is my child and that I'd missed out on the first four years of her life would affect me.'

'Nor me,' she said. She stood up from her desk and went over to the sitting area. Leaning against one of the armchairs, she looked at Jacques.

'We've got to get our feelings on an even keel before we involve Melissa. She's perfectly happy as she is so I don't want major disruptions to her life just because—'

'Is that what I am, a major disruption?' Jacques's eyes flashed dangerously.

He answered the shrilling phone on the desk. 'Dr Chenon here. Yes, Sister, I'll be along in a couple of minutes.'

'That was Sister on the medical ward. Claude wants to see me.'

'I'd like to come with you if you could wait a moment,' Liz said evenly.

Liz went over to the desk, glancing at the new blood-test results before making a note. There was no action that needed to be taken before the next morning.

Jacques stood up. 'Are you coming to see our patient in a professional capacity or simply because you want to carry on our discussion about Melissa after we've seen Claude?'

'Both. I'm off duty now, but I haven't seen Claude for a couple of days. I know he's not my patient any more but I feel a responsibility towards him, having been the one who admitted him to hospital.'

'And afterwards we could discuss Melissa's future, couldn't we?' Jacques said, holding open the door.

'And our own future,' Liz said quietly. 'We can't go on like this.'

'We certainly can't,' Jacques said as they began to walk down the corridor towards the medical ward.

Their patient was sitting in a chair beside his bed. Sitting next to him was his dark-haired wife.

'You remember Marie,' Claude said as the two doctors approached.

Liz smiled. She felt a glimmer of hope as she saw that Claude and Marie were holding hands. It seemed only a short time ago that Claude had poured out his heart to her and she'd realised that their marriage was going through a difficult patch.

'So, how can I help you, Claude?' Jacques began.

Claude smiled. 'I just wanted to say thank you for all you've done. I've had a whole day without dizziness or nausea and I can hear perfectly again. The treatment is definitely working.'

'That's wonderful!' Liz said.

'Yes, I'm really thrilled,' Marie said, smiling up at Liz. 'I must admit I had my doubts about the success of this treatment, but now I'm convinced. I'm so looking forward to Claude coming home and being well again. When will he be able to be discharged?'

'We expected to keep Claude in for a few weeks but as he's making such good progress I'm confident he'll be out sooner,' Jacques said.

'Thank you both,' Marie said, her eyes shining affectionately as she glanced across at her husband.

'It's not often that happens,' Jacques said as they went out through the ward door. 'It's great when you're called in to see a patient and all they want to do is say thank you. Makes it all worthwhile, doesn't it?'

Liz smiled. 'It certainly does. I'm delighted for both of them.' She hesitated. 'So, where are we going to have our discussion?'

'We could go back to my house, if you like.'

Suddenly Liz's pager beeped, indicating she had an urgent telephone call, and she and Jacques went straight to the nearest phone. *'Oui, Maman.'* As she listened to the voice of her distraught mother she turned pale.

'I'll be there,' she said, feeling as if she was in the middle of a bad dream.

'What is it, Elisabeth? What's happened?'

Liz stared at him as she hung up. 'It's Melissa. She's had an accident. She saw Mimi, our cat, running into the road and she ran after her and... Oh, Jacques!'

Liz buried her face against Jacques's chest as he pulled her into his comforting arms.

'Where is Melissa now? Is she...?'

Jacques felt as if he'd been stabbed through the heart. His daughter, his precious little girl, the daughter he hadn't known he'd had. Just when he'd found her she was being snatched away from him.

'They've called for the ambulance. Melissa should be in A and E as quickly as they can get her here. Maman says she's still breathing but… It was a car. The driver said he never even saw her until it was too late to stop and then…'

'Oh, no!' Jacques was fighting back the tears as the two of them clung to each other.

Liz wiped her eyes as she looked up at Jacques. As parents, she felt they'd finally bonded, but at what a cost. It was so sad that it had taken a dreadful crisis to bring them together again. Only when they'd realised what they might have lost…what they might be losing…

'Jacques, I couldn't bear it if…'

Jacques tightened his arm around her shoulders as they rushed down the corridor, two distraught figures, united in their grief, both of them oblivious to the inquisitive glances that came their way.

Sister Catherine came towards them as they reached A and E.

'I know you're off duty, Elisabeth, but there's a little girl being brought in by ambulance and—'

She stopped as she studied Liz's tear-stained face. 'Why, what's the matter? Is there…?'

'It's my daughter who's being brought in,' Liz said.

She wiped a tissue over her face and pushed her hair back behind her ears as she forced herself to become calm again.

'Our daughter,' Jacques said, with the emphasis on the word 'our'.

Catherine was utterly perplexed but didn't want to pry. Nothing ever surprised her nowadays. She'd noticed that Elisabeth and Jacques had seemed close but she hadn't known they'd had a child together!

Liz could hear the sound of the ambulance siren. She

hurried to the front door, running outside to stand by the closed doors of the ambulance. Why were they taking so long to unlock the doors? Come on, come on…

'We must stay calm,' Jacques said, putting his arm once more around Liz's trembling shoulders.

'I'm OK now,' Liz said in a shaky voice.

Beyond the ambulance she could see Clive's car pulling up. Her brother-in-law leapt out and came over towards her.

'We've done everything we can, Liz. Your mother and sister are in the ambulance with Melissa.'

A paramedic was opening the ambulance doors from the outside.

'Maman!' Liz held out her arms towards her weeping mother who was now stumbling down the steps of the ambulance.

Mother and daughter clung to each other briefly before Liz moved to look at the tiny figure on the stretcher.

She swallowed hard, trying to remain calm as she viewed the unconscious body and deathly pale face of her beloved daughter. Even the light tan that Melissa had acquired as she'd run along the beach seemed to have vanished.

Liz bent down, kissing the dark strands of hair that lay tangled across the top of the stretcher as she reached for her daughter's chubby little wrist, feeling for her pulse. There was no blood, no stain on the white sheet, no apparent injury on the surface of Melissa's skin. But underneath…?

Were there internal injuries? A subdural haematoma in the skull, perhaps putting pressure on Melissa's brain? That would account for the fact that Melissa was still unconscious.

A kindly paramedic touched Liz's arm and told her

that he'd been monitoring Melissa's pulse during the journey. It was very faint but it was still there. The little girl was holding her own, though why she was still unconscious was yet to be diagnosed.

Liz thanked the paramedic for his help but insisted that she wanted to check Melissa's pulse herself, wanted to do everything she could to save her daughter. But as she felt for the pulse she realised that she was trembling so much she couldn't make any kind of accurate assessment.

Jacques tightened his grip on her shoulders. 'Wait until Melissa has been taken inside,' he said gently.

An elderly man was pushing through the medical team outside the Clinique. 'I want to see the little girl's mother,' he said anxiously. 'I want to tell her—'

'I'm Melissa's mother,' Liz said, her hand still on the side of the stretcher.

The man's face crumpled. 'I'm so sorry, dear. I never even saw your little girl. She seemed to come from nowhere. I wasn't going very fast. The first I knew was when something seemed to bounce off the side of the car. I stopped as soon as I could and there she was, lying in the road. Poor little lamb. She's going to be all right, isn't she? I've got children and grandchildren of my own, so I know what you're going through....'

One of the nurses had taken hold of the man's arm as he dissolved into tears.

'I'm sure it wasn't your fault,' Liz said, as she watched the distraught man being led away.

As they entered A and E, Charles Grandet, the doctor in charge of the intensive care unit arrived. He had been called in by Sister Catherine to make an assessment of Melissa's condition.

'I believe Melissa is your daughter, Elisabeth,' he said in a kindly tone.

'And mine,' Jacques said evenly.

Dr Grandet's eyes didn't even blink at the unexpected announcement. Sister Catherine had already told him some garbled story about a romance but until Jacques Chenon had confirmed it, he hadn't thought it credible.

'I'm going to take Melissa up to Intensive Care,' Charles said gently. 'So, if you'd both like to follow me...'

Jacques put out a detaining hand. 'Charles, Melissa needs a CT scan as soon as possible. We've got to find out why she's still unconscious. There could be a subdural haematoma, in which case I would want to operate to relieve the pressure.'

Charles Grandet leaned towards his colleague. 'With respect, Jacques, if we do need surgical intervention for your daughter, I think we should call in an expert in brain surgery, don't you?'

Jacques swallowed hard. 'You're probably right. But, Charles—'

'Jacques, you and Elisabeth are understandably overwrought. It's a terrible trauma when your child is involved in a traffic accident. May I suggest that you stay here in the hospital, but leave the hands-on work to the rest of us. You're too emotionally involved when it's your own child.'

My own child! For a moment, Jacques allowed himself a shiver of excitement at the thought that he actually had a beautiful daughter. But for how long? Looking down at the tiny slip of a girl clinging to life, he felt he couldn't bear it if he should lose her now. Now, when she didn't even know he was her father.

He put out his arm and drew Elisabeth against his side. 'We'll come with you to Intensive Care, Charles,' he said in a subdued voice. 'But you'll get that CT scan done as soon as possible, won't you? And you'll alert the surgical team if you need to follow up with the removal of—'

'Jacques, stop worrying, it's all under control,' Charles said in a soothing voice.

'What time is it now?' Liz said, wriggling herself into an upright position in the armchair beside Melissa's bed.

'It's almost four,' Jacques said, standing up and stretching his arms.

'In the morning?'

'Yes. You've been asleep but not for long.'

Liz realised that she must have slept for about half an hour, but she was feeling refreshed. Refreshed but still desperately anxious.

She leaned over her daughter. Melissa was completely silent but the tubes and wires attached to her were still bleeping quietly. She glanced up at the cardiac monitor. A good steady heartbeat now. So why wasn't Melissa regaining consciousness? Why was she still in that twilight world from which she might never emerge?

The CT scan had revealed that there was no haematoma beneath the skull, pressing on the brain. Liz remembered the relief she'd felt when the surgical team had been told they wouldn't be needed.

She touched Melissa's pale cheek. 'Melissa, come on, darling, open your eyes. Mummy's here. Mummy and Daddy.'

She looked across at Jacques.

He leaned across from the other side of the bed and took hold of Liz's hand.

'Nothing else matters, does it, Elisabeth? So long as our precious daughter lives I'll never ever complain about anything again.'

Liz gave him a loving but wry smile, leaning across

Melissa's bed so that she could brush her lips across his cheek. 'Oh, but I think you will, Jacques. You'll find something to complain about. Just as I will. We're only human, after all.'

Jacques nodded as he clung to her hand. 'You did so well, having our baby by yourself. I wish I'd been there but I understand why you didn't feel you could contact me.'

'Do you, Jacques? Do you really understand the dilemma I was in?'

He nodded, not daring to speak for a few moments in case his emotions got the better of him again.

'And I'm sorry you've missed so much of Melissa's life,' Liz said gently. 'I can fully understand why you felt angry.'

'I'm not angry any more, Elisabeth.'

He looked down at their unconscious child. 'She's so beautiful, Elisabeth. Just like her mother.'

'But more like her father,' Liz said softly. 'The dark hair, the impulsive, mischievous…' She broke off as one of the nurses came in to check the monitors.

'Is there anything I can get you, Elisabeth? A cup of coffee perhaps?'

Liz shook her head. 'How about you, Jacques?'

'No, thanks.'

The nurse went away. They were once more alone with their daughter.

'I hope Maman and Gina are OK,' Liz said, leaning back in her chair. 'Clive took them home soon after we admitted Melissa into Intensive Care. I said I'd phone in the morning if there was any change.'

'There wasn't any point in them staying,' Jacques agreed quietly. 'I had a word with the man who was driving the car while you were with your mother. He was anxious to speak to one of Melissa's parents and I thought it might be better if I saw him.'

'He seemed such a nice man. What did he say?'

'He said the police had interviewed him, as well as your mother and sister. Between them they'd formed a picture of what had actually happened. Apparently, Melissa had been playing with the cat in the garden. The cat suddenly ran out through the gates and Melissa shot after him, shouting at him to come back.'

'And that's when the car came round the corner, I suppose.'

Jacques nodded. 'The man said he heard a thump on the near side of the car and…'

There was a choking, coughing sound from Melissa. Jacques leaned across and removed the oxygen mask from his daughter's mouth.

Melissa stared up at Jacques. 'I would have caught Mimi if the car hadn't been there.'

Melissa's voice took them both by surprise. Her eyes were flickering open. She was trying to rub them but the tubes and wires were making it impossible.

'Melissa, darling!' Liz leaned over to hug her daughter.

'Mummy, I've been asleep. Where's Mimi?'

'She's at home, Melissa. She escaped to the other side of the road.'

'Did she? I'm glad she's safe. She was very naughty. She shouldn't have run out of the gate like that. She might have been run over by that car. I remember I tried to jump out of the way and then…then… Where am I?'

'You're in the hospital,' Jacques said, squeezing his daughter's hand as he sent up a silent prayer of thanks.

He'd made such a fuss about claiming her and had then spent days sulking because he hadn't been allowed to be part of his daughter's life sooner. But from now on he wasn't going to waste any more time.

'Melissa, there's something your mother and I want to tell you,' he began tentatively.

Melissa gave a cheeky smile. 'I know what you're going to say. I had a sort of dream a little while ago. I was kind of sleeping and then waking, but it was too much effort to open my eyes so I just listened to what you were saying.'

'And what were we saying?' Liz asked.

'You were saying that Jacques is my daddy...*mon papa*!'

Liz's eyes held Jacques's from across the other side of the bed.

'And what do you think about that?' Jacques asked nervously.

'I think it's great! I've always wanted a proper daddy. You are my proper daddy, aren't you, Jacques? Not just a pretend one?'

'I'm your real, proper daddy,' he said, his voice husky as he choked back the emotion.

'For ever and ever?' Melissa tried to lift herself up but the effort was too much. She leaned back on the bed. 'Promise you'll always be there, Daddy.'

'I'll always be there, Melissa.'

Liz was reaching for her tissues again.

'I think I'd better check you out, Melissa,' Jacques said, standing up and reaching for his stethoscope.

Suddenly, he felt capable of functioning again as a man and as a doctor. The events of the past few days had temporarily knocked all the stuffing out of him but, looking at the two wonderful girls in his life, he knew he was fully recovered.

CHAPTER NINE

LIZ ran up the shore and flung herself down on the towels they'd spread on the sand. Jacques had already rubbed himself dry. He lay on his side, propped on one elbow.

'We haven't got long before the others arrive,' Liz said. 'We ought to go in and start making lunch.'

Jacques put out a detaining hand. 'It's all arranged. My domestic help, *ma femme de ménage*, who lives in the village, is coming in for a couple of hours this morning. She's a very capable woman. The kitchen will be spotless, the vegetables will be prepared.'

'I'll go in and spike the lamb with garlic and rosemary and make sure the oven is hot enough,' Liz said, standing up.

Jacques patted the towel beside him. 'Sit down, Liz. We'll both go in together soon. I'm glad you came early so we could have a swim but I want to have you all to myself for a little while longer. I've got something very important to ask you.'

Liz smiled as she curled her damp legs beneath her. It was a warm day so she didn't feel cold but she wanted to have time for a shower before her family arrived.

'My mother said we needed time to ourselves. That's why she suggested bringing Melissa along later with Gina and Clive.'

'It's been a long couple of weeks,' Jacques said, 'since that awful night when we didn't know whether Melissa was going to live or die.'

'She's made an amazing recovery.'

'We all have,' Jacques said, smiling. 'It's not long since we were dwelling on the past instead of concentrating on how lucky we are. When we nearly lost Melissa it was almost as if it was a punishment. I felt as if we didn't deserve to be blessed with our beautiful daughter.'

'And we didn't,' Liz said. 'We were simply accepting that she was there. Not realising that she was the most precious gift of our lives.'

'Talking of our lives, we haven't discussed our future,' Jacques said, his eyes registering a deep tenderness. 'Elisabeth, will you marry me?'

Liz's heart thumped. Being married to Jacques was something she'd always dreamed about. Marriage, being parents to Melissa, living the rest of their lives together. It was all too wonderful to contemplate. Such a big step forward, such a wonderful adventure!

Jacques put a hand on her arm. 'You don't have to give me an answer until you've really decided what—'

'Oh, yes, Jacques, I've decided.' Liz's eyes were shining as she turned her head towards him.

She moved into the circle of his arms, snuggling herself against him, wanting to become part of him.

'If I seemed hesitant just then,' she began, 'it was because I was overwhelmed by the enormity of the last few weeks. Finding you again, almost losing you when we quarrelled, then almost losing Melissa. And then the joy of you and me being reconciled. But marriage…'

'Are you trying to stay that marriage is a step too far? Are you afraid that…?'

'Jacques, marriage is the most perfect ending to the first part of our lives. And the most perfect beginning for the rest of our lives together. Jacques, I love you so much.…'

Jacques's arms tightened around her as he kissed her tenderly at first, and then as the need for consummation surged through him his kiss deepened....

Liz sighed with ecstasy as Jacques's caresses aroused the sensual areas of her body that craved his touch.

'Jacques, we mustn't. Not now!' Liz pulled herself away, running a hand through her tousled hair as she tried to bring her senses under control again.

Jacques sat up, trying to calm his vibrant body. They had both been reaching the point of no return. Liz was right to call a halt at this point. The wonder of knowing that she was going to be his wife had removed all sensible thoughts from his mind. He only knew that he wanted to make love with Elisabeth to celebrate the unbelievable fact that they were going to spend the rest of their lives together.

'Listen, I think that's the sound of a car in the drive.' Liz jumped up, slinging her towel around her shoulders.

'Will you stay afterwards, after they've gone?' Jacques said, his voice husky with emotion. 'I actually phoned Gina to see if she'd take care of Melissa tonight so that you could stay.'

Jacques took hold of Liz's hand as they ran into the garden through the little gate at the edge of the beach.

'I know, she told me.' Liz smiled. 'She said I ought to stay with you because we hadn't had any time to ourselves for the past couple of weeks since Melissa's accident.'

Jacques squeezed her hand. 'So, is that a yes? You'll stay?'

Liz smiled. 'Of course I'll stay.'

'Maman, Papa!' Melissa was running over the grass, her little arms outstretched. '*On va nager?* Can we swim?'

'*Chérie*, Maman and I have already been swimming and it's nearly time for lunch,' Jacques told his daughter as he swept her up into his arms and swung her around. 'But we'll swim again this afternoon.'

Melissa's arms tightened around her father's neck as she begged for more swinging around.

'Encore! Encore, Papa!'

Liz smiled affectionately as she put her hand on Jacques's arm. 'You'll both be dizzy if you don't stop. Let's go inside. I need to shower and change out of this wet bikini as soon as I can.'

'I'll give everybody a drink while you're changing,' Jacques said.

'Thanks.' Liz kissed the side of his cheek. He'd pulled a pair of jeans over his swim shorts, together with an old fisherman's jersey. The effortlessly casual clothing, coupled with his tousled black hair and tanned body, made him look so handsome.

'You look like a swarthy Mediterranean fisherman,' she whispered into his ear. 'Soo sexy! I could really fancy you.'

He caught hold of her wrist. 'I'm sorry, *mademoiselle*. I am soon to be married to the most wonderful girl in the world.'

Liz giggled. 'Just my luck!'

Jacques gave her a rakish smile. 'But if you would like to come out in my boat this evening...'

'Come on, Daddy,' Melissa said, tugging at his hand. 'Let's go and do the drinks.'

Jacques blew Liz a kiss over the top of their daughter's head as he allowed himself to be taken into the house.

Liz ran up the outside stone staircase at the back of the kitchen. She needed a few minutes to herself before she faced her family. She was trying to remain calm but the excitement of her forthcoming marriage was colouring all her thoughts.

As the warm water of the shower cascaded over her she wondered if every prospective bride felt as she did. That she was the only girl in the world to have ever been married.

As she stepped out of the shower she conceded that although she wasn't the first girl to marry she was the only girl to be marrying the most wonderful man on earth.

Liz crossed the lawn, smoothing her hands over her white cotton skirt, pulling down her skimpy pink top so that it wouldn't reveal too much of a gap. The girl in the shop in St Gabriel had assured her yesterday that with her narrow waist she could carry it off perfectly, but Liz had worried that the outfit might be a bit young for her.

When she'd gone into the kitchen just now, the *femme de ménage* had assured her that lunch was nearly ready. Everybody was having drinks in the garden.

'Liz, you look radiant!' Gina whispered as, champagne glass in hand, she moved out of the gazebo to greet her sister.

Jacques followed close behind Gina to put an arm around Liz's waist. 'What a transformation from the wet, sand-covered girl who dashed inside to take a shower!'

He lowered his voice. 'You look beautiful, darling.'

'Doesn't every bride?' she whispered back.

Gina smiled. 'I heard that. Have you two got an announcement to make? I've saved half a glass of champagne just in case.'

Jacques smiled. 'I brought up a whole case of champagne from the cellar this morning. I was hoping we might have something to celebrate.'

Karine moved to join the small group by the entrance to the gazebo. 'And do you have something to celebrate, Jacques?'

Jacques was holding his hand over a champagne bottle as the cork eased itself out. 'Yes, we do have something to celebrate. Let's drink a toast to Elisabeth, who has agreed to be my wife and make me the happiest man in the world.'

He poured out a glass for Liz before raising his own glass towards her. 'The bride-to-be!'

'The bride-to-be!'

As the toast echoed around the garden, Liz could feel the tears pricking at the backs of her eyes. She couldn't believe she'd come through the turmoil of revealing the truth to Jacques. Their relationship had not only survived but strengthened.

She raised her glass towards him. 'To the most wonderful man in the world!'

Melissa was tugging at her mother's skirt, her eyes round with amazement. 'Is Daddy really the most wonderful man in the world?'

'He is for me,' Liz said.

'And me!' Melissa said, cautiously raising her glass of orange juice, careful not to spill it, as she'd seen the grown-ups do.

'To my daddy, the best daddy in the world! Oops! Sorry, Mummy!'

With the hand that wasn't holding the glass, Melissa tried to brush away the splash of orange juice that had somehow jumped out onto her mother's new white skirt and was spreading a stain.

Liz smiled down at her daughter. 'It doesn't matter, darling.'

Nothing mattered except the fact that the three of them were a real family at last.

'More champagne, Gina?' Jacques said as he circulated with the bottle.

'No more, thank you. I'm limiting myself to one glass today.'

Liz glanced at her sister. 'Are you driving, Gina?'

'No, I'm driving,' Clive said, smiling as he stood up. 'That's why I'm on orange juice. Gina and I have got something to announce as well.'

Liz stared at her brother-in-law as she waited. 'Go on, Clive, don't keep us in suspense.'

It couldn't possibly be what they'd all been hoping for, could it?

Gina's smile broadened. 'I'm expecting a baby...at long last!'

Liz felt another surge of happiness as she hugged her sister. 'Gina, that's wonderful. I can't believe it!'

'Neither can I!' Gina said. 'I'd almost given up hope! Ten years of marriage and no baby!'

'Well, it wasn't for want of trying!' Clive put in, with a broad happy grin on his face.

Gina laughed. 'That's why I thought it wasn't going to happen. I think having Melissa around the house has helped me to relax. When I looked after her by myself I began to feel like a mother. And then, hey presto! Here I am, eight weeks pregnant.'

'It's going to be lovely, having another baby around the house,' Karine said.

'Will it be a girl, Aunty Gina?' Melissa asked.

'I don't know, darling. I really don't mind.'

'I don't mind either,' Melissa said. 'So long as I've got somebody to play with.'

Melissa looked up at Liz. 'And you and Daddy could

have a baby, couldn't you? Mummies and daddies do get babies, don't they?'

'Yes, they do. But when you start school, you'll have some new playmates,' Liz said quickly. 'At the *école maternelle* you'll have lots of new friends your own age.'

'And you'll be able to bring them home to play with you,' Jacques said.

He was looking at Liz over the top of Melissa's head as he continued talking to his daughter. 'Mummy and I haven't decided where we're all going to live, but I think…'

Liz was nodding. She knew exactly why Jacques was looking at her with that enquiring expression. They hadn't discussed it but Jacques had realised that she already loved this house.

'I think we'll be living here,' Liz said. 'It already feels like home to me.'

'And me!' Melissa was dancing up and down, laughing as she made up an impromptu song. 'I'm going to live in a castle, I'm going to live in…'

The little girl broke off and looked up at her father. 'If I live in a castle, does that mean I'll be a princess?'

Jacques smiled. 'You'll always be my princess, Melissa.'

'So you'll be king and Mummy'll be queen.'

'That's what it will feel like,' Jacques said huskily.

'I'm going to go in and check on the lunch and make sure everything's ready for our trip tonight,' Liz whispered to Jacques.

He put his arm around her waist. 'I think you'll need a hand….'

* * *

'Elisabeth, do you realise that since you came back to France this is the first time I've managed to lure you onto my boat by yourself?'

Liz leaned back against the side of the boat, trailing her hand in the water as she lazily watched Jacques steering the boat with his bare foot on the rudder. The low slanting light from the sun was dazzling her even with her sunglasses. She half closed her eyes. That was better.

'You sound as if you're planning a seduction.'

Jacques laughed. 'I am.'

'Good! I haven't had a real seduction for…let me see…'

'Five years?'

'Mmm!' Liz giggled. 'That was the best seduction I ever had. Only thing was, it can't be a real seduction if you're both planning to seduce each other.'

'And were you planning to seduce me that evening?'

'Only after we started walking on the sand. And then I felt it was written in the stars that we should be together.'

Liz moved across and sat beside Jacques. 'I feel exactly the same tonight. Hurry up and park the boat and…'

Jacques laughed. 'Park the boat! What kind of an expression is that to use with a seafaring captain? I'll have you know, young lady, I come from a long line of seafaring folk. My great-grandfather was a pirate.'

'Rubbish!'

'No, really—well, sort of!' Jacques was shielding his eyes from the low rays of the sun as he made for the little cove where he'd taken Elisabeth on their last excursion at sea.

'I've no idea how the old rogue made his money, but he was a simple fisherman, so the story goes, and one day he returned from a long voyage with enough money to buy himself a plot of land, build a house and retire.

Not a lot of money, but enough to set tongues wagging. He was a good, honest type apparently, so the family never did know how he came by the money.'

'If your great-grandfather hadn't decided to stop fishing, you might have still been a fisherman,' Liz said, standing up to uncoil the landing rope.

She stood at the edge of the boat, ready to throw it ashore when the boat was close enough to the shore.

'I could have been happy as a fisherman,' Jacques said. 'So long as I'd had the right woman in my life. Somebody a bit like you.'

He cut the engine and, grabbing the rope from Liz, he leapt ashore to tie up.

'A bit like me?' Liz said.

Jacques smiled. 'Well, perhaps a lot like you.'

He held out his hand towards her. As she stepped ashore, he grabbed her around the waist, pulling her against him.

'May I say, you parked the boat beautifully,' he said, running his hands lightly down her back.

She groaned in frustration. 'Jacques…don't tease me. Make love to me…now…!'

As she opened her eyes and stared up at the stars Liz couldn't think where she was. There was the sound of the waves, the smell of the sea close by. She turned to look at the pebbles glinting in the moonlight, at the motionless figure lying on his back, arms spread out like a child's, smiling at something in his sleep.

They'd hardly stopped smiling and laughing during the night. For a short time after they'd driven each other wild with passionate embraces and tantalising, erotically stimulating caresses they'd become serious. But as soon as they'd regained their breath, there had been more laughter, more excited talking about the wonderful future ahead of them. Then, inevitably, more kisses, more caresses, more love until, satiated and exhausted, they'd fallen asleep in each other's arms.

Jacques opened his eyes and pulled her against him. 'It's too late to sail back home tonight. Would you like supper or breakfast on the boat? Take your pick because the sun will be rising in a couple of hours.'

'Both, but let's sleep first in the cabin,' Liz said. 'And then when we wake...'

'When we wake I'll throw in a line and catch you the biggest fish in the Mediterranean. We'll grill it for breakfast and eat it sitting on deck in the morning sunlight.'

Jacques broke off. 'I've never been so happy in my entire life, Elisabeth. Thank you for coming back into my life...and bringing Melissa.'

He leapt aboard and held out his hand. She clambered into the boat after him.

'We'll need a bigger boat soon, for Melissa and her friends to join us,' Jacques said as he led the way into the little cabin.

Liz smiled. 'The joys of being a parent!'

'Only just starting,' Jacques said as he began letting down the bunks that were stored in nets slung from the roof of the cabin. 'Would *madame* prefer a double or two twins?'

Liz gave a contented smile. 'What do you suggest...?'

CHAPTER TEN

THE village church was packed. It was standing room only and many of Jacques's and Liz's friends and colleagues had chosen to stay outside in the warm sunshine. Although it was the end of September, it was still hot in this sheltered part of the Mediterranean coast.

Walking back down the aisle, feeling the swish of her satin skirts around her, Liz paused for a moment as she felt a slight tug from behind. Melissa, helped by two of Jacques's older nieces, was dutifully clinging hard to Liz's lace embossed train. But somehow the little girl had managed to step on the delicate fabric and was now being pulled along in the folds.

A laughing Jacques turned round and lifted his daughter, holding her safely in his arms as he continued to walk with his new bride towards the church door.

Everybody surged forward as the bride and groom appeared. Melissa, clasped in her daddy's arms, waved ecstatically.

'This is such fun, Maman! Will you get married again?'

Jacques and Liz laughed. Their eyes met above their daughter's head.

'I certainly hope not,' Jacques said quietly, as he leaned forward to kiss his bride on the lips.

The photographers were positioning a group of relatives beside the bride and groom. Melissa was persuaded to have one photograph taken standing in front of Liz's skirts, holding her own little bouquet of roses, which had been retrieved from the aisle where she'd dropped it at the beginning of the ceremony.

'Qu'elle est adorable, la petite!'

The guests clearly found Melissa delightful as they watched her smiling at the camera in between her almost non-stop bursts of chatter.

Liz was aware of a blur of faces in front of her as she posed for seemingly endless photos. She had no idea she had so many relatives! At the civil ceremony the previous evening, she'd been introduced to cousin after cousin and numerous aunts and uncles. Some of the relatives were on her mother's side, down from Paris. A small number of relatives on her father's side of the family had flown in or driven down from England.

But by far the most numerous section of relatives was from the Chenon family.

Jacques was taking Liz's arm now, hoisting Melissa up on his shoulder as they made their way through to the waiting car. Once the three of them were settled on the back seat they relaxed.

Jacques turned to Liz and kissed her. The cameras flashed from outside the car. Liz smiled through the window. They were moving. A moment or two to themselves. Was there time to talk to Jacques about...? Probably not. Later...

Liz smoothed her hands over the ivory satin of her skirt as she looked down to check that the tiny buttons of her bodice were still fastened. The delicate pearl buttons had taken ages to fasten that morning because each one had to have a loop around it. On the way to the church, the top two buttons had unlooped themselves as she'd leaned forward. Maybe her bust was getting bigger? No, it was too early for that, wasn't it?

'You look wonderful, Elisabeth,' Jacques said softly.

He felt a little tug at the sleeve of his black jacket.

'And so do you, Melissa.' He bent to kiss his daughter's cheek. 'You look so pretty in pink.'

'Can I take my dress off now? It sort of itches round my neck and I'm all sweaty.'

'Keep it on for a little while longer,' Liz said. 'Grandmaman is bringing a cotton dress you can change into when—'

'There's the restaurant!' Melissa said, excitedly. 'Oh, look, they've still got the Bouncy Castle like they had when we came here for lunch with Pierre. He's my daddy's daddy, isn't he? So does that make him my grandpapa?'

Jacques smiled. 'It certainly does.'

'Good! I like Pierre. Grandpapa Pierre...and there's my new cousin Jacqueline...Jacqueline! *Attend moi! J'arrive tout de suite!*'

As soon as the chauffeur opened the door of the bridal car Melissa escaped over the grass towards the children's play area. Clutching her frilly skirts above her knees, she almost made it before falling over on the damp grass.

'Oops!' Melissa pulled herself to her feet. The green stripes on her pink dress looked quite pretty really. She turned round to see what her parents thought.

Mummy and Daddy were waving from the restaurant door. Asking if she was OK. They seemed to like the green stripes as well.

Melissa grinned. 'I'm fine!'

'Are you sure you don't mind only having a two-day honeymoon?' Karine whispered in her daughter's ear as she prepared to say goodbye. 'I can take care of Melissa for as long as you want to stay away.'

Liz smiled. 'We're happy with two days. Next summer

the three of us will take a longer holiday somewhere…probably,' she added lightly, hugging her secret to herself.

Who knew what would have happened by next summer? The three of them might be… She hesitated. Should she tell her mother? She would be over the moon, but she wanted Jacques to be the first to know.

She kissed her mother on the cheek. Karine thought she'd never seen her daughter look so happy. But her going-away clothes were unusual to say the least! She'd never seen a bride and groom leaving their wedding reception in jeans and sweaters before! Jacques and Elisabeth must be the least conventional couple in the world but they certainly seemed the happiest. It had all turned out so well for them.

'Have a wonderful honeymoon, Elisabeth,' Karine said, as she tried unsuccessfully to hold back the tears.

Everybody was crowding around now, trying to say goodbye to the bride and groom.

'Lovely wedding… Beautiful ceremony… Fabulous reception… Have a wonderful honeymoon…!'

The voices were ringing all around her as Liz bent to kiss her sleeping daughter who was being carried out to one of the waiting cars by Clive and Gina. Melissa had been asleep for the past hour, snuggled in a blanket on a sofa in a corner of the room, totally oblivious to the loud music and the chatter of the people dancing near her.

Liz had made sure she had explained to Melissa that she and Jacques were going away for a couple of days. From the moment Melissa awoke in her own bed she would be well cared for.

Pierre was waiting by the door. 'Goodbye, Jacques. Take care of your beautiful bride.'

He kissed Liz on the cheek. 'Welcome to the family,

my dear. I'm so glad you and Jacques decided to have the reception here.'

'Here, where it all started,' Jacques said huskily. 'If Elisabeth had cancelled her table that night…' He broke off. The awful thought was too much to contemplate.

Pierre put his hand on his son's arm. 'Oh, fate would have found some other way to get you two together. You were made for each other. And if it's written in the stars, it will happen. It just might have taken a bit longer, that's all.'

Jacques put his arm around Liz's waist. 'It took too long as it was. Come on, let's make up for lost time.'

Everybody cheered as the bride and groom hurried out to the waiting car.

The chauffeur, a friend of Pierre's who'd known Jacques since he was a child, closed their door after ushering them in, before resuming his place at the wheel.

'Where to, Jacques?'

'My boat, Bertrand. It's on the far end of the beach, tied up at the jetty there.'

The chauffeur started the engine. 'Why isn't it in its mooring place in the harbour?'

Jacques smiled. 'Because Elisabeth and I want to walk on the beach first.'

The chauffeur shook his head. 'Now, why would you want to do that?'

'Don't worry about it, Bertrand.'

'You'll spoil your shoes. The sand will be wet.'

'We'll take our shoes off,' Liz said.

The chauffeur gave a sigh of resignation. 'Well, if you're sure that's what you want. Haven't you got any luggage?'

Jacques smiled. 'There's a box of stuff on the boat.

We won't need much. We're only going away for a couple of days.'

Jacques put his arm around Liz's shoulders and drew her against him. 'Only a couple of days on the boat,' he whispered. 'Are you sure this is what you really want, Elisabeth? We can have a proper holiday next summer, just the three of us.'

'We might want to change our plans by next summer,' Liz whispered. 'I've got something to tell you. I only found out myself this morning and I haven't had you to myself long enough to…'

Jacques was holding his breath. 'Tell me, tell me…'

'I did a pregnancy test just before I left for the church this morning. It was positive.'

'Oh, my precious darling!' Jacques folded Liz in his arms.

Liz sighed happily as she looked at the approaching lights at the edge of the beach.

'I thought I had everything,' Jacques breathed. 'But now I know I've got the most perfect honeymoon gift….'

The chauffeur was holding open the car door.

Jacques clutched Liz's hand and together they ran across the deserted beach in search of the warm rock where they'd first made love….